ALL MY LOVE, FROM THE TRENCHES

ALL MY LOVE, FROM THE TRENCHES

REILLY VORE

NEW DEGREE PRESS

ALL MY LOVE, FROM THE TRENCHES

ISBN 978-1-63730-430-3 *Paperback*
978-1-63730-517-1 *Kindle Ebook*
978-1-63730-518-8 *Ebook*

For Allan and Don, my spirited grandfathers who both served and loved the earth so well. Samuel belongs, in part, to you.

And for Nancy and Carol, my strong grandmothers who always spoke their hearts and minds. The gumption of both Nellie and Lillian came through me but ultimately from you.

CONTENTS

AUTHOR'S NOTE

Dear readers,

History is not simply a compilation of facts, but a looking glass through which to examine people and their relationships. This looking glass is one into which I have found myself falling like Alice—curiously, willingly, and excitedly. History is like a treasure hunt—a constant search for what people (and their lives) were like. Each new fact, each new moment where we see a piece of their world, comes with the realization they are not so different from us.

I have discovered through my study of history those who came before are not the flat characters we loathe. They do not stay the same—much like we do not stay the same. We can watch them transform throughout their lives. They are changeable. History and historical figures are breathing, complex, and not that different from us. In fact, we exist purely because they lived and lived well. So why wouldn't we want to know them? Why wouldn't we want to explore their worlds? To follow the treasure hunt of facts and figures is to reach back and pull truth through the folds of time. What a gift that is.

While nonfiction texts and biographies can show us real, tangible insight into these people, I think historical fiction can help us to understand their lives in an inviting way. It pulls us into the past slowly, and before we know it—we're invested. Historical fiction has always held a place in my heart. To put it simply, historical fiction can hold all the wonder and timelessness of the past without the pressure to remember what we read for a test later. It can feel like a more accessible way to examine history. We can find ourselves rooting for characters in another time—almost forgetting any differences completely. The ability to examine historical moments through the lens of fiction is a magical thing.

World War I is the moment I chose to examine in this novel. The four years of the war resulted in so many changes. This war brought about the roaring twenties—a generation attempting to forget the horrors they saw. It began closing the gap between classes. It ushered in mental health strides with the discovery of PTSD (then known as *shell shock*). The role of women shifted significantly in many ways. This war was important. But the people living it did not know the beautiful impact they had. They did not know the strides they would make. They were simply trying to do their best—living through one of the most destructive periods of time. They are living proof that great change can occur when we think it might just be another step forward.

This is not a history book. This is not a textbook. This is an examination of life in another time. These characters are like you and I. They dream, they struggle, they fall in love, they work, they fear change, they look toward the future, and more. This is true to historical figures. They are not so different. I wish to show these fictional characters living through real moments in time are not unlike real historical figures, and, even further, they all are not unlike us. Both my characters and the real people of the time are simply people making choices, living their lives, and trying to do their best.

Samuel Perry, the gardener boy, struggles between the duty to support his family and the overwhelming desire to defend his country. He accepts the love his employers give him but is constantly aware of the economic divide that separates them.

Lillian Harlow, the headstrong socialite, is in her own battle with societal expectations for a woman of the time as she yearns to be valuable to those she loves. She speaks her mind, suffers the consequences, and looks forward to the changing world in front of her.

These two characters, along with several others, show how each person is different and responds to the war in their own way. These times, like any other, have no clear answer, no clear path, and demand each person to come to terms with their own reality and decide how long their status quo can truly be maintained.

Fiction and history blend together so we can keep interacting with it. We must remember the moments that came before, improve on the moments to come, and recognize the significance of both.

So here it is—a fragment of my heart dancing across history.

Here are my characters—people of then—who are presented to you, the people of now.

I hope you will find pieces of your own soul in them, and they will show you the importance of their world to examine your own.

All my love,
Reilly Vore

CHAPTER 1

Samuel Perry's father had been dying for a week. The influenza swept through England, and few people did not know someone who witnessed the sheer depth of its grip. Samuel Perry had heard rumors in the street of how quickly it could take hold, but he never imagined it could cling to the walls in his own home.

At first, Samuel had watched his mother, Anna, nurse his father's fever for three days with no sign of it breaking. The steady decline had been hard for Samuel, who had to confront this new reality.

Eleven years they had lived in the tiny home just a short walk from the Harlow country estate where his father worked as the gardener. His younger sister, Nellie, was nestled in the corner of their parents' small bedroom, watching the scene. Samuel caught himself staring at the littlest Perry and admiring her growth since their arrival. How she had changed from the eight-year-old child to the nineteen-year-old young woman who sat before him. She looked small with her petite, spritely features and her pale skin. He wondered what would become of them both if their father did not recover.

Suddenly, that question demanded an answer when William Perry's chest heaved for one last heavy breath. His eyes never opened again.

Silence loomed over the tiny household and stood next to each member of the trio as they realized only they remained. Samuel's mother rose from the bedside slowly with William's sweat still on the rag she held close.

"Samuel, run to the Harlow's. Tell them your father—" Her voice halted. Samuel could visibly see his mother's broken heart forbade her from speaking. He hugged his mother and squeezed her hand as he turned to leave. The sudden, final close of his father's life shocked him to his soul. He just witnessed his father's last breath—something he thought he would be doing twenty or thirty years from now.

His daze continued as he left his home and walked toward the Harlow residence. Samuel's mind bounded on, racing toward the inevitable realization he had to leave them. All of them—the Harlow family.

The Harlows had become an extension of his own family since his father became their gardener when Samuel was thirteen. Frederick and Mary Harlow were the kindest of employers. They praised his peonies and rained admiration on his roses—each the purest pink in the county.

When they learned William Perry had two children, they insisted the children come occupy their own. Samuel and Nellie felt as if their birthdays and Christmas had fallen on the same day. In one moment, they went from living in a small, rickety home to one of the largest estates within forty miles—the kind that had at least eight fireplaces, high ceilings in every room, and swords hanging in the library. In addition, they were granted the company of new friends who became almost family in a matter of weeks.

The boys of the family had welcomed Samuel with open arms. Daniel was four years his senior and James only one, although James often acted older. Both boys had their father's look. Daniel was always considered the handsome one, with his dark chocolate curls and deep, amber eyes. What James lacked in blatant handsomeness he made up for in wit. His eyes were lighter than Daniel's—certainly his mother's influence—but his curls were as envied as his brother's. John was the youngest of the Harlow boys, a full six years younger than Samuel. John inherited his mother's looks but all his father's stubbornness. His hair was the color of hay, and his eyes rivaled the greenery Samuel's father tended. Samuel noticed when he was young John resembled him more than his own brothers. The four boys were together so much of the time others usually assumed he was one of them. As the years passed, Samuel began to feel he was.

Samuel turned his memory to his favorite Harlow. Lillian had always been his favorite. She was the female equivalent of Daniel. Unsurprisingly, the pair of them consistently had suitors and sweethearts falling at their feet and baring their souls and being trampled by the next. Lillian appeared to have endless grace—which she did, but she could rival any of her brothers and Samuel in a footrace and would climb higher in a tree than any dared. The little wildflower for which she was named matched her soft gray eyes. Lillian once told him her parents intended for her to be called *Lily* for short, but he was the only one who did. She enchanted her parents, but of course they yearned for the day she would finally be settled. Her mother insisted on manners and ladylike behavior from her only daughter. Instead, she had gumption—which Mary endlessly told her was highly unbecoming. But Lillian never relented.

Samuel and Lillian raced often and talked even more. Lillian would steal books from Frederick's personal library to sneak to Samuel. Lillian took no interest in books, but the pair would run to the top of the furthest hill on the westward side of the Harlow property and Samuel would read aloud. As they grew, he found himself remembering those moments the most. He would read to her about Dorothy Gale and Sherlock Holmes. Once, shortly after Lillian had turned sixteen and had started entertaining suitors, he read her *The Awakening*, and he blushed three shades darker than his father's flowers when Edna removed her clothes. Lillian only became enraged a woman could be so saddened by such a small man.

"I would never love such a weasel!" she screamed.

Samuel chuckled, slowly relieved of the red, and just gazed at her. She stopped pacing and looked back at him. He stared like he was seeing her as a young woman for the first time rather than a playmate. Samuel watched the blush change faces and jump to her cheeks. But as he remembered himself and his station, his eyes returned to the stolen book.

Samuel rummaged through an endless string of memories as his feet carried him down the familiar walk to the Harlow's. Years passed since then. Daniel and James had each gone to university to study business and medicine, respectively, which left Samuel behind, but never alone. Their constant letters were his favorite companions. Samuel knew he had to write to them both and tell them the news about his father. The walk was increasingly painful as the death of his father punched him in the chest with every step forward.

Lillian was now twenty-one years old and no longer ran or climbed, but she displayed her competitive nature each time she turned down a marriage proposal another girl had undoubtedly been yearning for.

"Who's the poor bloke this month?" Samuel asked her every now and again. He would smirk and watch her eyes roll, but he knew she almost wished for the teasing so she could punch his arm or push him—a small moment of contact they were rarely granted.

"Don't be silly," she would scoff. "I don't seek them out. They just . . . find me."

Then he would roll his eyes as she had.

Samuel was twenty-four years old and had become a man in the eleven years since he'd met the Harlows. He now towered above Lillian, and his shoulders had broadened and arms strengthened from helping his father with his work. His skin was suntanned, which often betrayed him—he was not a member of the wealthy inner circle. But he caught Lillian admiring the glow on more than one occasion.

A screech from down the lane startled his memories away.

"Sam!" the little voice cried. "Sam, I'm coming with you!"

Samuel turned to see Nellie sprinting down the road after him. Nellie and Lillian had grown together naturally as the only girls in a swarm of brothers. Samuel enjoyed watching the two young women in his life together. He knew Nellie loved the Harlows as much as he did, and she was rarely seen out of their company.

"Why aren't you at home? I'm not leaving you out. I have to go tell them we're leaving," he almost shouted.

"I know. Which is why I'm coming. If you get to say goodbye, so do I."

She was headstrong like Lillian. Normally, he would be annoyed by his sister's insistence, but he was secretly relieved he didn't have to face the Harlow family alone.

The two siblings walked the rest of the way in silence until they reached the Harlow estate. Samuel gripped the large, elaborate lion door knocker and knocked three times. Each time the knocker met the door, it echoed into the night until it settled and covered the Perry children in silence once more. He felt Nellie's gentle hand slip inside his own calloused one, and they stood that way—still as statues—until the door opened.

It was the early hours of the morning. The family was not even awake. At four o'clock in the morning, the Perry children were there before their father was even expected. But ever faithful, the Harlow butler, Mr. Taylor, welcomed them with surprise. The elderly man stood tall and grand. His hair was peppered with gray and experience, and his demeanor was often stern. However, Samuel and Nellie both knew he had always been fond of them.

"Hello, Mr. Taylor."

"Samuel, Nellie—what are you doing here at this hour?" He sounded concerned, as if he knew something grim was about to darken the sunshine the day promised. Samuel raised his head to meet his eyes, and Mr. Taylor said no more. He asked no more questions and asked for no explanation. Instead, he moved aside and allowed Samuel and Nellie to walk into the grand house together—their hands still intertwined.

Samuel led Nellie into the foyer but held her in place, refusing to go any farther. Mr. Taylor left in a blur and went up to wake Mr. and Mrs. Harlow. The moments that followed both flashed and skated by in slow motion before Samuel's eyes, his body enduring every pang of reality and grief. Frederick Harlow came down first, with Mary fast on his heels.

"My dear boy, what's happened?" Mr. Harlow asked in his low, slow voice. Samuel felt Nellie's hand go limp and heard her cry beside him for the first time, as if the question made their father's death real.

"Sir, our father, he's—he's just passed." Samuel's voice faltered, but he stood tall. His new position as provider fell heavier on him with every word he spoke.

Mrs. Harlow gasped and scooped Nellie into an embrace and led her away to the parlor. Meanwhile, the two men stood together—mere feet away—with a chasm of silence between them.

Suddenly, Samuel caught sight of a soft, yellow robe floating down the stairs like a bird in flight. Catching his eye from her place at the top of the staircase, Lillian raced to Samuel and wrapped her arms around his neck. He raised his arms to catch her. With his height, her feet barely touched the floor.

Frederick Harlow left the pair to speak to Mr. Taylor across the room. Lillian's grip tightened around Samuel and her chin sank into his right shoulder. Once Samuel realized the sweet moment had gone on for too long to be considered appropriate, he set her down immediately. Her hands fell away, but one stayed—resting on his forearm.

"Samuel, I—I'm so sorry. We all loved William," she said.

Samuel just nodded, afraid if he spoke, he would cry. He had never cried in front of Lillian before, and he was reluctant to start. Her soft eyes met his—a full conversation took place between them, though they stood in complete silence. The trance was broken suddenly with the return of her father, and Lillian's hand jerked away as if it had never been there.

"Samuel, I have a proposition for you," Frederick started. Samuel glanced at Lillian for some kind of sign of what was coming next, but her face held the same confusion. "I know nothing can comfort you in this time, but what are your plans moving forward?"

"Sir, my father passed moments ago. I haven't had time to think, let alone make inquiries. However, I'm sure we will have to stay with family elsewhere until I can provide for my mother and Nellie." From the corner of his eye, he watched his sister's head snap up. All at once, the house fell silent. John Harlow broke the quiet by sprinting down the stairs like Lillian had.

"Samuel, no!" he screamed. "You can't leave. Daniel and James are gone. You can't leave me here alone with Lillian."

Mrs. Harlow grabbed her youngest child's shoulders and pulled him backward. Even at eighteen, Mary Harlow babied him and chastised him more frequently than any of her other children.

"How kind of you to think of the Perry family in this time rather than yourself, John," she snapped. Her grip tightened on his shoulder until he was quiet and sitting next to Nellie.

"Samuel," Mr. Harlow started again. "I want to offer you a position here. I want to offer you your father's position. No one knows our land as well as you, and nobody could do your father's legacy justice as you could."

Lillian looked up at him, waiting for his answer.

"Sir, you can't possibly mean it."

"I'm quite serious."

Samuel cried in front of Lillian for the first time.

CHAPTER 2

The days following the death of William Perry were seemingly endless for Samuel and the Perry women. Samuel had watched the influenza take the light from his father's eyes and the house, but also bring some light back in.

The lone Perry man spent the morning of his father's funeral walking the grounds his hands loved so well. His thoughts constantly turned to wonder how one man could have cherished land that was not his own for so long. He yearned to do it justice—to do him justice.

The morning mist hung in the air around Samuel as he wandered through the endless greenery. The sun had already risen high, but the dew declared a somber day—as if it knew. When the sound of two competing motors met his ear, his head whipped up from the gardens. He lowered his head again to his work with a smirk because he knew the occupants of each cab were competing just as fiercely.

A weight lifted from Samuel's burdened shoulders when the cars stalled in front of the Harlow estate. From the garden on the edge of the house, he saw the two oldest Harlow boys, his brothers, racing from their respective vehicles. He marveled at how different Daniel and James were even in adulthood. Where Daniel had allowed his curls to grow long—no doubt as a result of traveling so much—James cut his short so only the ends showed he had any curl at all. Daniel wore a full suit in all his seriousness, while James only wore his trousers, tailored shirt, suspenders, and a smile. Samuel could even see James' eyes flash a look of sheer competition as they met Daniel's copper ones.

The Harlow boys had raced to his side in the wake of the tragedy that left him a man alongside them. Daniel's feet hit the ground with a heaviness Samuel now knew all too well. Whether the oldest Harlow knew it or not, their bond had been strengthened when Samuel became responsible for the Perry family—just as Daniel would one day be for the Harlow family and everything with it.

Each Harlow aggressively shed the layers of their lives as they ran toward their friend. When Daniel's jacket hit the ground behind him, Samuel's eyes wandered to his other companion, who practically run out of his shoes at least thirty yards earlier. James ran with all the freedom Daniel lacked, and Samuel watched the fighter in his eyes as he set the pace. He knew James would make it to him first since Daniel had to beat him in every other event life had to offer.

He watched the two boys shed their responsibilities and convention with every step toward him—the gardener boy. The grass still crumpled under their feet the same way it had when they were young.

"Samuel!" James' voice rang out first. He was the closest to Samuel in age, and they had always bonded over their admiration for the single Harlow girl. James had always been Lillian's favorite brother—she told Samuel this many times. Although, it would always come with the threat of passing Samuel off as a liar if he breathed a word of it to the other two Harlow siblings. Samuel had always felt the closest to

James and Lillian. The other siblings of either family could rarely infiltrate the bond, but they also had little desire to try.

"Samuel!" shouted Daniel, the eldest Harlow. Samuel had the luxury of loving Daniel like a brother but not envying anything he possessed, because he knew he would never have it. The ease of their relationship would never quite take root in the relationship between Daniel and James. Samuel knew every step toward him brought them closer to their brother who had the privilege of not being born a Harlow.

Samuel stood slowly from the ground as he witnessed his childhood years rushing toward him across the deep green grass. The midday sun had betrayed him again, and his light shirt now hung close to his back as his sweat secured it in place. He raised one arm to his forehead to block the rays in time to see his companions a mere foot in front of him. Laughter exploded from Samuel's throat as the Harlows mowed him to the ground he had been working from.

He sprawled with one brother on each side and his limbs every which way, as if the skies opened and dropped him from above. He climbed to his feet and extended one arm to each brother. Daniel and James grabbed onto him and stood, ignoring the perspiration that was even more evident than before.

"Samuel, did you honestly grow again?" Daniel asked.

Samuel smirked. Daniel was once the oldest and the tallest brother, but time had cheated him out of the latter position. Samuel stood stiff as a board. His broad shoulders placed his head higher than either of the Harlow boys.

"At least one foot," he spit back.

The banter sank back into their bones like they had never been apart. James' sturdy hand landed around his shoulder while Daniel took his other side, and the three sauntered toward the house. Samuel wondered if they realized they interrupted their employee's duties as they ushered him inside, but it seemed in this moment he was more brother than gardener. With all the Harlows, sometimes the lines blurred.

The trio rounded the corner the two boys had come from and took one large stride through the front door. As they entered, Lillian descended the stairs the same way she had the night of William Perry's death. She scurried to her siblings the same way she had to him only days ago. Her arms flew around each brother, which left her face deeply embedded in the middle of the huddle in Samuel's chest. Her grip tightened for a moment, and Samuel wondered if it was for her brothers or for him.

"Daniel, you need a shave. James, Mother said you couldn't arrive until tomorrow." Samuel watched Lillian perform her sisterly duties—each word proving her status and driving the wedge further between her world and his own.

"When I heard Danny was coming today, I had to beat big brother home. Never mind the footrace I just beat him in," James said with a full smile.

Daniel's eyes rolled as he grabbed Samuel by the neck and ushered him further inside. Mary and Frederick greeted them all, beaming at their boys. Feeling amazingly out of place in the grand room with high ceilings, silver set out for tea, and a chair that could most likely pay his home's rent for three months, Samuel tried to escape. But when he turned, Mrs. Harlow caught him and set him firmly in the chair—securing his place in the conversation.

Samuel watched Lillian position herself strategically in the chair opposite him. The two of them were famous for the faces they would make through conversations they had little interest in. Usually, Samuel found they existed in their own realm that only tangentially touched reality. He looked at his former playmate and saw her as the woman she had become. She was twenty-one years old, had men falling at her feet, and yet she chose to talk to the gardener still—after all these years. He would never understand her.

Talk swirled about James and his life in the medical world. Mary Harlow beamed with pride when he spoke of the babies he delivered in the middle of the night or the surgeries he brilliantly executed. Lillian rolled her eyes, and Samuel caught the expression with his own chuckle. Daniel paced back and forth in front of his chair for the hundredth time in twenty minutes.

"Son, when are you going to stop traipsing the globe and come home to learn what you'll actually have to do when I die?" Frederick Harlow rarely spoke bluntly, but this he said with a bellow.

Both Daniel and James lowered their heads—both clearly annoyed at the interruption. Even Samuel had grown uncomfortable as his employer's eyes pierced Daniel.

"I've told you. I'm traveling while I can. You should be thankful I've made it back at all."

"What do you mean by that remark?"

"Only that something's coming," Daniel said, looking at his logical younger brother. "When I was traveling back from Poland to be here, the only thing anyone could talk about was Germany. How they've gotten stronger. How they now hold the Ottoman Empire."

"Nothing will come of it. Why are you talking like this? Are you trying to scare your mother? Or avoid the conversation we constantly have to keep having? I've told you to stop this foolish gallivanting, but you never listen to me."

Samuel watched the scene, considering what his comrade said. The Ottoman Empire had fallen to Germany. Suddenly, he felt the shifting sands on which his world sat. He felt Lillian's eyes on him, but his were focused on Daniel. A million thoughts filled his head, making it almost physically heavy. The weight drew his eyes to the floor until the moment had come for his departure. He rose slowly.

"I really must continue the work outside." Samuel bowed to the Harlow parents, smiled at James and Daniel, and flashed Lillian a frightened look before exiting.

His feet rushed him through the foyer and back out to his plot where the boys found him. He did not have to rise again to know the footsteps following him belonged to Lillian.

"What is it? What do you know?" His eyes caught hers again.

"There's talk everywhere, Lily. I thought the others were off. I thought they couldn't be right." He knew he couldn't possibly be making sense to her. He was still trying to sort words into sentences as they fell out of his mouth. "Men downstairs, the footmen, Taylor—they all say Germany is getting too high and mighty. Say they're taking too much. Say we'll have to do something soon."

He watched her watching him. She was waiting for some kind of better answer than the one he had given, but only silence existed between them. The girl and the gardener stood face-to-face—unmoving.

"Who's *we*?" Lillian asked. But the answer hung in the air between them.

Samuel and Lillian locked eyes again—now standing only a mere two feet away, but both feeling the distance that was sure to come soon.

"England. Daniel, James—" he started. "Me."

* * *

Samuel sauntered back down the lane toward home to collect his mother, sister, and the only suit he owned. The funeral had been arranged for the late afternoon, so the majority of his work would be done. His father would not want him to miss a day of work—even if it was for his funeral. With Daniel and James returning home, all the talk of Germany and the potential for war, and his discussion with Lillian, he had almost forgotten he had to face burying his father as well.

He arrived at his little home to find Nellie sitting in the corner—in the same place and the same way she had sat the night William Perry died. He strode past her to his room to change out of his sweat-soaked shirt and his dirt-stained trousers. As he buttoned his jacket, he watched his sister. She only changed her position when he finally moved toward her.

"Sammy, I don't think I can do it," she said. No tears slid down her cheeks, and her voice never faltered—it was simply a fact. Samuel knew what she meant. He felt the same, but he also knew he did not have the luxury of not believing he could lay their father to rest. As the man of the house, he was meant to be the strong one. But when his sister looked up at him, he knew she saw her grief reflected in his eyes.

"We'll do it together, Nel. You, me, and Mum." The reality of their missing member sank through the air like a stone into water. Samuel sat by his sister and waited for Anna Perry to emerge from the room that now only belonged to her. Moments later, the Perry mother joined them, wearing black and age that had not been visible until a few days prior. Samuel had never seen it on his mother before. Grief had advanced the years for all of them—not just him.

The trio walked to the cemetery and William Perry's resting place. They met the minister and the entire Harlow family. Mary Harlow let go of her husband's arm and folded Anna Perry into her hug. Frederick Harlow turned toward Samuel, shook his hand, and followed his wife to stand by his mother.

Each Harlow boy followed suit, shook their companion's hand, and turned to stand behind the family. Samuel immediately felt out of place, as this was the only time he'd ever stood in front of the Harlows as if he took precedence.

The minister began speaking about his father and his life and the family he left behind, but Samuel didn't hear one word of it. He stood tall, but certainly not strong, and let his shoulders rise and fall as he held each tear firmly in his throat—refusing to let them exit. He could hear Nellie's tiny sobs and his mother's hands fumbling around the family Bible she held—as if somehow clinging to it harder would change their reality.

The service ended as quickly as it began, for which no one was more grateful than Samuel. He stared into the ground where his father now lay.

"Samuel, I'm so sorry for your loss. Please write if you need anything," Daniel offered, shaking his hand once more and leaving. James and John nodded behind their brother, implying a similar sentiment, and turned to follow him away from the cemetery. Samuel watched the Harlow parents say their goodbyes to Nellie. His sister finally turned from Lillian's embrace to offer a hand to their mother—decidedly forfeiting her own grief for the sake of their mother. The Harlow parents followed their sons while Nellie led Anna Perry back toward their home. Exhaustion spread across each of their faces. Samuel turned to face the only Harlow left—Lillian.

"Samuel, I—I'm so sorry. I don't know what else to say." Lillian reached for Samuel's hand but quickly retracted as Mary Harlow yelled for her from down the road. Samuel watched Lillian turn to face her mother and wished her hand had met his—even when he understood why she stopped herself. It was impossible for him to wish for what he did. He knew that.

"Thank you for coming. Your mother is waiting," he said as he backed away. He turned to follow his mother and Nellie, but Lillian grabbed his hand and pulled him in tight for a hug like she had the night his father died.

He wrapped his own hands around her and held her until she stepped back to hurry after her parents. He watched her walk away, waiting for her to look back, but she never did. He half smiled as he thought about how the things they stole together had changed as they grew—from books to embraces. But the smile faded as he wondered what would be stolen from them both in the days and weeks to follow. So Samuel followed his family down the lane—unsure of what kind of world would be waiting for him.

CHAPTER 3

Lillian's brothers stayed for three days after William Perry's funeral. She constantly found herself wondering how all six of them once lived under the roof of their estate. She knew Daniel and James had not seen each other in months, and her older brothers undoubtedly were even more competitive when under the watchful eye of her parents.

Her father's attention was turned to Daniel and his reluctance to stay at home and learn the management of the estate. Meanwhile, her mother constantly asked James about what surgeries he had done, what lives he had saved, and more. She watched contentedly. She welcomed her brothers mostly for the distraction, because it meant her mother wasn't so constantly focused on Lillian's marital status.

The day of her brothers' departure, she woke knowing her parents' gaze would once again shift to her and her rebellious younger brother. It was perhaps the only moment of Daniel and James' visit she wished they would stay longer. As insufferable as they could be, she wrote them enough about their mother's interference. They were happy to take the attention away for a time. She watched the cars come around to the front door as she stood next to James, and they waited for the rest of the family to come say their goodbyes.

"They didn't see, you know," James said with a nudge of his elbow and a smirk.

Lillian's head snapped up to face him. The color drained from her face. Her brother's teasing eyes danced as they met her own. She nudged him back and returned her eyes to the ground with a smile.

"How did you see?" she answered, attempting and failing not to sound panicked.

"We were walking so far ahead after saying goodbye to Samuel, so I turned to see if everyone was following—you weren't."

"I was just . . . comforting him—paying my respects."

"Yes, I'm sure he was comforted," he said with another big brother grin that made Lillian boil.

She punched him like she had a million times when they were young. She could not decide whether to laugh or fear somehow her parents would discover their moment through James. She opened her mouth to reject his assumptions or deny what the moment was or meant, but each attempt fell flat in her mind as she waited for him to speak. Instead, Lillian was startled back to reality by her father's voice behind her.

"James, talk some sense into your brother."

"He can't force me back here any sooner than you can." With this parting remark, her eldest brother stepped around their father and went directly to his car. He was gone faster than he came. She wondered if the constant pull of her father's expectations would one day be the death of Daniel. She knew he could not avoid the family duty forever, but she admired his efforts. She only wished she could do the same.

James followed Daniel's example and strode to his own car. Lillian wished for another moment with her brother to explain the scene he saw, but instead, he only grinned at her through the window and drove away. Lillian stood statuesque, watching him leave, and hoped he would keep her secret.

* * *

James' letter arrived almost a month after his departure. Lillian opened it quickly and muttered words throughout that her mother would scold her for if she heard them. But relief flooded her. Her secret would remain a secret.

Dear Lillian,

I know you must be worried I've told either Mother or Father what I've seen. But I think what you've failed to understand is I have not told them anything for years. I'm not blind, Lillian—and you're not subtle. You never were. Of course you'll deny what I'm assuming are feelings for him, but whether you admit them or not, your secret is safe with me.

Of course you know they would never approve. It is not the way the world works—not for people like us. You'll have to accept a proposal at some point, or you know they will undoubtedly accept one for you. Promise me you'll make a choice soon. I don't want to see you alone, and alone in a marriage is worse. Daniel would take care of you when he inherits, but God knows neither one of us wants to owe anything to the one who gets everything and wastes it.

I'm not sure if what he said at home is true, but I don't doubt that soon we will all be asked to determine what is worth fighting for. Either with war or with the people we choose. Please be certain it's worth it—whatever fight you take on.

Your affectionate brother,
James

* * *

The days and weeks following the visit of her brothers brought a tension to the house. Each head turned whenever a telegram would arrive or the telephone would ring. Each person in the Harlow estate down to the kitchen maid heard what Daniel warned. No individual or country had envisioned the toppling of the Ottoman Empire.

Each week after the arrival of James' promise brought another letter, but they were almost always for Samuel. Lillian pretended not to notice the constant string that came and went. She wished talk of war would stall and the correspondence would cease altogether. She knew war would inevitably take both the sender and the recipient of the letters while her role would be unchanged. Each man in her life would leave if war came. Samuel, of course, had relinquished one or two of the letters, but not one brought her ease.

Only one letter he showed her replayed over and over in her mind until it became as much a companion as the one who received it. It had come from Daniel. It was short, to the point, and the most frightening of all.

Dear Samuel,

I'm not sure what's coming for us. James and I have spoken more in the past few weeks than we have in the last year. We have a plan if war comes. We'll enlist—both of us. Naturally, your decision weighs heavier than ours. But we've been almost brothers in every other way, so why not brothers in arms? Think about it.

Daniel

She could feel him watching her read, but she had only raised her head after reading the letter a dozen times at least. His lips moved, ready to speak, but she silenced him.

"It won't come. Europe is more peaceful than ever. It won't happen." Lillian's sentences sped out of her mouth—one right after the other—like she couldn't contain them. She paced back and forth until she paused, waiting for a reply.

Samuel glanced at her, and he only nodded. She wasn't sure if what she said was true or if she was warding off some kind of evil most of England already accepted was on the horizon. Whatever the truth, she shoved the letter into his chest, and his hand rose to catch hers. No words were spoken—only another nod from Samuel—and she withdrew her hand and left him.

When the newspaper arrived at the Harlow residence, Lillian met Mr. Taylor at the bottom of the stairs and stole the letters and newspaper off his tray quickly.

"Miss Lillian, I would give the paper to your father." He spoke plainly and firmly, which only made her want to open it. But, fearful of its contents, she did as she was told and handed the crisp parcel to her father.

"Dear God," her father said as she sat beside him. "The Austrian archduke has been assassinated." He sprang from the table but left the paper, which Lillian stole and read for herself. As much as she claimed Europe's peace was long-lasting, the news that morning said otherwise.

Not one member of the household spoke at breakfast, and it was one of the only meals for which Samuel and Nellie sat at the Harlow table. Her mother ushered them in shortly after the news broke. The unspoken understanding that something was coming hung in the air next to the crystal chandeliers and peered down at the group. The silence was deafening, and Lillian watched Nellie drown in it beside her. Suddenly, Nellie sprinted from the room and out to the grounds that certainly felt safer somehow.

Each member rose from the table as silent as they ate and exited until only Samuel and Lillian remained. The world must have truly gone mad for her mother to leave her alone with a man. She spoke first, as she often did.

"What will you do—if war comes?" He let her read Daniel's request, but they never discussed his answer.

"You mean when, I think," Samuel said.

Lillian moved from the table to the large window that overlooked the gardens Samuel tended. His handiwork was easier to look at than him.

"*When* war comes . . ."

"Daniel and James would answer the call. No doubt in my mind. You saw his letter. They've known for weeks they would enlist. I know what I think is the right thing to do. But I don't know if I have the luxury of choosing to die the same way they do."

The mention of death, specifically Samuel's, made Lillian return to the table. She leaned over Samuel, and he shrank in his chair, resembling the boy she met so long ago.

"Don't you dare. Don't you dare talk about dying. And don't you dare play the martyr. I apologize you don't have half of what we have. But you've seen my brothers and even me feel trapped by the 'luxury.' One brother wants the inheritance, one doesn't, and they're not in the correct birth order to get their wish. John is aloof and fighting every day with someone, and I'm waiting to be sold to the highest bidder because I can only turn down so many men before Father picks one for me. So don't you dare talk about the *luxury* of dying. Because this is most definitely not a luxury."

Lillian stormed from the room, leaving the dust of her words to settle in front of Samuel. She would not cry in front of him, and she refused to hear him talk about death for another moment. She knew he would feel awful. Only a few times in her life had she properly scolded her friend for his words, and never over something as serious as war. Every word was true. None of her brothers were happy—not one, and Lillian, as independent as she was, could only stay that way for so long. Samuel had that choice at least. The ability to choose his life. The choice to leave or stay, and mostly she was worried she already knew what he would choose.

The days after the assassination loomed heavily. The summer that once was filled with picnics, parties, and solitude seemed to be filled only with worry and waiting. Even the debutantes felt a shadow cast over their special days. July burned with little solid word on what was next for the country, let alone Lillian or Samuel. But on the morning of August 5, 1914, like so many other events in the house, troubling news came with a crash under the cover of night.

The knocks became increasingly more desperate as the seconds passed. Mr. Taylor rushed to the door as quickly as his bowed legs could carry him. The bangs might as well have been cannon fire. They echoed throughout every room in the house.

Mr. Taylor opened the door cautiously, and Frederick Harlow was only a few steps behind. Lillian, John, and their mother had emerged but only moved a few feet since the knocking increased.

Daniel Harlow stood disheveled on the doorstep with worry in his eyes. Lillian watched her father and brother speak silently with a million glances until her father led Daniel into the library. She followed them until her brother's eyes met hers at the top of the staircase. He shook his head slowly before the tall, oak door closed with an echoing bang. She raced down the stairs but was left frustrated by the thickness of the library door. Somehow eavesdropping felt easier when she was a child.

"Lillian! Come away. This is between Daniel and your father," Mary Harlow whispered.

"Oh, Mother, I think we all know this is between us and Germany," Lillian spat back.

Silence.

Lillian could wait no longer. Her feet led her faster than her mind as she entered the room and stood still as a statue. Mary only half attempted to stop her daughter, and she followed with John stumbling behind. Glances between the five Harlows all spoke the same word: *war.* A simple nod from her father was enough to send Lillian to the floor. Their entire nation had dreaded this moment, and suddenly, the room seemed darker. Lillian's nightgown felt like mourning clothes.

"James is on his way to enlist." Daniel spoke with no emotion—only facts would serve this conversation. "I mean to join him when I leave you."

Every head snapped to attention. Lillian's eyes moved to her mother, who was watching her son and perhaps realizing only now he was a man. Frederick Harlow nodded and exited.

"I'm going too!" John yelled behind him as if he was joining a game of hide and seek.

Lillian stayed motionless but gazed at her oldest brother, knowing this would not be the last goodbye. She rose slowly, kissed Daniel's cheek, and returned to her room, leaving her mother a moment alone with her oldest son.

For Lillian, the day had begun—she knew no sweet relief of sleep would return for the rest of the night. She instead fell to her knees once more—this time by her bed. She knew she should be praying for the country, Daniel, James, and perhaps even John to remain home. Instead, she only uttered one sentence for one man.

"Don't let him go."

CHAPTER 4

Samuel sat outside of his home considering the severity of the world in which he now lived. Before news of Franz Ferdinand arrived, he would spend the evenings inside with his mother and Nellie—talking about their days, laughing about nearly anything. But as his world slipped further into the chaos that was spreading across Europe, more of his nights were spent in solitude.

The summer night was damp but cool. The air felt as heavy as the weight on his shoulders. He had spent the summer writing Daniel and James. With each letter, he both feared and anticipated news of war, but none ever came through the correspondence.

He knew Lillian also awaited each new letter. At first, he had told her when the letters came, but as her demeanor changed, they met each new letter with his muddled excitement and her obvious dread. Eventually, he instead stuck each one in the bag of his father's tools in the Harlow greenhouse. He had only shown her one—the one from Daniel asking him to enlist with them if war came. Immediately he regretted pulling the letter from its hiding place as he watched her face fall. She had gripped the letter tightly until she shoved it back toward him, retreating to the house.

The roar of an engine interrupted his thoughts. The car blew past him and suddenly stopped with a blast that sounded like a gunshot. He stood quickly—wondering who was going to emerge from the vehicle and why it should be in front of his quiet home so late. His protective stance lessened when Daniel stepped out of the vehicle and ran to him almost like he had the day of his father's funeral. Oddly enough, Samuel saw the same thrill in his eyes, but it was tainted with the smallest glimmer of worry.

"Sam, it's here. It's happened. We're at war! James and I are going to enlist. We'll have to wait until morning, but we're meeting soon after I tell the family. We'll wait as long as we have to for the office to open. Come with us, please."

Samuel's thoughts swam, but not a single one came up for air to create a response for Daniel. Instead, he stood in the street, alone with his friend, knowing no one in the town or even the county probably knew yet what he did at that moment.

"Go," he said. "I'll follow you first thing." Samuel could barely see Daniel in the night, but he heard the grin in his voice when he spoke.

"This is it, Sam. This is what we've been waiting for."

And with that, he disappeared up the lane to the Harlow estate.

* * *

Samuel remained outside and watched until Daniel arrived at the Harlow estate. He knew in his heart war had arrived, but his mind remained in the darkness of night—still fogged in the reality he had committed to enlisting with his adopted brothers.

Morning broke more quickly than normal. He had hardly slept since telling Daniel he would follow after them. In truth, he would have gone to meet James right then if his family had known. He owed them an explanation, although he was sure the engine of the car had woken them. He also knew he owed it to the Harlow family. Their kindness could not be met with a retreat—even an honorable one. Samuel walked quietly to the estate—replaying every moment of the short conversation he knew changed his life—even if he didn't yet know how much. He watched each man pass him with a look of determination on his face and each woman with pure worry on hers. He knew, as he continued toward the Harlow estate, another look of worry would surely meet him.

Samuel walked up the familiar lane like he had so many other times before, but this time was different. For the first time since his father's death, he could not be sure what would occur when he reached the front door. Each step led him further into the unknown until he finally reached the greenhouse. He was sure the Harlows were expecting him to make some appearance inside on a day as changeable as this, but his morning solitude was essential. His watering came first, then the tending, transplanting, new planting, and more until he turned to find Lillian among the blooms. Each time she met him in his little haven, he acknowledged how at home his friend with the floral name stood in the hot rooms.

"I looked all over the grounds for you. I've been awake since dawn," she said. He knew she must have woken with Daniel's arrival, and he could be almost certain her eyes did not close for the rest of the night.

"You found me."

"Daniel came last night to tell us. We're at war, Sam." Lillian moved closer to him. "They're both going to enlist. Even John is going. Mother is hysterical. Father is beside himself with joy at raising three dutiful boys, and quite frankly, I'm baffled at how we all got here." She spoke one fragment right after the other with hardly a breath in between.

Samuel ran his gloved hands down the rosebush he was planting and rested them on the shelf in front of him. He knew in that moment Daniel had said nothing of the promise he made to him the night before.

"Will you go? You won't go, will you?" Desperation and worry glittered in her eyes, the kind Samuel witnessed in the other women he passed on the way to work. Undoubtedly, they were asking their men the same question.

Samuel looked up at her slowly and wished with every part of himself he could give her the answer he knew she wanted. But before he could give her any answer at all, a motor's roar snatched their attention away. Lillian turned before he could speak, and the pair stood at the door of the greenhouse.

And Samuel wanted to know what it felt like—enlisting on the brink of war.

The world slowed to a halt as he stood behind Lillian. His arm rested above his head on the door frame—blocking the morning sun. He watched Daniel and James exit the car with John on their heels. Lillian turned, smirked at him like she always had, and shifted away as the boys moved closer—now only a few yards in front of them.

"James, what happened? Did you all enlist? When do you leave?" Lillian's questions flew from her mouth. Samuel wanted the answers as much as she did.

"We decided to come back—didn't feel right going without Sam," James said with a grin. But Samuel watched the words tumble from his mouth and knew the destruction they would soon cause. "It's time to go."

Samuel's anticipation turned to dread as the words fell from James' mouth. All at once, he knew what they had done. He heard Lillian's breath catch. She pulled up her skirts and pushed through her trio of brothers to sprint toward the hill.

Without thinking of how his actions would appear for perhaps the first time in years, he left Daniel, James, and John where they stood and followed Lillian. He called her name more than once, but her stride never slowed. Samuel wished he would have told her his decision the minute she found him—told her Daniel came to tell him first. He finally caught her when she reached their hill—their hiding spot from parents and responsibilities for so much of their youth.

"Lillian, wait," he gasped.

"How could you not tell me? You let me ramble on in the greenhouse and ask if you were going. You already knew! You decided you were going the minute Daniel's letter came." Her words dripped with frustration Samuel could feel. He stood slowly from his stooped position and met her gaze. He waited to speak, hoping her demeanor would change, but she stood indignant as ever, waiting for a response.

"I hadn't decided when Daniel's letter came," he said boldly. "But last night before he came to the house, he stopped by. He told me they were going to enlist. He asked me to go, and I told him I would follow this morning." He stood like the soldier he would soon become.

"You should have told me."

"I was going to. When we got back." Lillian's head hung low and shook back and forth. Samuel could see the words she was trying to form. He wondered what would come next. Lillian was changeable and unyielding, so it was unclear where the next moments would take them.

"I mean so little to you that you would not even ask me how I felt about you enlisting?"

"I don't believe it is a requirement as your employee to request your permission to take up arms, Miss Harlow." His words surprised even himself. Lillian stepped back as if his statement physically pushed her.

"No, Mr. Perry," she spat back, "it is not. But I thought you might value my opinion as my . . . friend." She retreated.

"It wouldn't change anything, Lily," he called after her. His voice made her pause but not turn toward him. Instead, she crossed her arms and strode toward the house, leaving Samuel unsure of where they stood. The way she had staggered on the word *friend* would stay with him the whole walk back to the greenhouse where the Harlow boys remained—waiting for him.

"What was wrong with her?" John asked. Samuel glanced at James, whose eyes spoke volumes, and asked a string of similar questions.

"She was just upset about you—all of you. She's worried for your safety."

Samuel wasn't sure any of them believed a word of it, but they brushed off their cares and climbed into Daniel's car. It was one of the only times in Samuel's life he had been in one. The interior was smaller than he imagined, but the laughter of the three brothers made it feel large and full. Each voice grew as they talked about enlistment, physicals, training, war, glory, and what their next weeks would look like. Samuel felt a guilty excitement as the car sped away.

"Sam," Daniel started. "We were worried you would stay. I'm glad you're coming with us."

"Oh, stop being soft!" John almost yelled. "This is it. This is what I wanted. We'll all leave and come back heroes."

"I don't think it happens quite like that, John." James laughed.

"Maybe not for you. I plan on fighting harder than half the British army, old man," John continued. Laughter erupted as the brothers shoved each other and dreamt of glory and spoke of the war that would surely be resolved in a matter of months.

Samuel watched Daniel—tall, unchanging, and prepared for whatever might come. Then his eyes shifted to John—headstrong, unyielding, and foolish. Then to James—solemn, determined, and calculated. Finally, he looked out the back window of the car toward the Harlow house. He imagined Lillian standing in the dust of the car, and he wondered what her role would be as he rode closer to his own.

CHAPTER 5

James sat in the car marveling at his three companions. Daniel seemed almost as giddy as John the closer they sped toward enlistment. Samuel joined in with the occasional comment but often sat quietly. After witnessing Lillian's moment with Samuel at the funeral, James had often wondered if his friend reciprocated the feelings he clearly saw in his sister. Samuel's sprint confirmed it. His brothers had exchanged confused glances, but James was never more sure—the attachment was obvious. A man ran after a woman for only two reasons: to apologize or to catch her, and Samuel had spent his youth running alongside Lillian.

"It won't last. No one thinks so, but we'll all get to say we were part of it," Daniel said.

"And I'll get to shoot something better than Father's old guns," John said with a grin.

James rolled his eyes at the ignorance of the youngest Harlow while hoping the eldest was right—that it wouldn't last too long. War was something all young men dreamt of—a way to escape. But he often wondered if the escape would be worth it or if they would all want to escape that too. While Daniel and John spoke of their dreams of glory and guns, James turned to Samuel.

"Is she alright?" he whispered. But Samuel simply shook his head in reply. He wasn't sure what their conversation consisted of, but he rarely did. Samuel wouldn't likely divulge the details of one of this magnitude, but it was worth a try.

A slow rumble silenced their chatter as their vehicle screeched to a halt. They finally arrived. James looked out the window at the masses that formed in the street. It seemed as if all the men from at least four counties had the same notion they had. The car could not even come within a mile of the line with the crowd that had formed.

"I'm going now. Follow if you want to actually go to war this year," John shouted as he bolted from the car. The smallest Harlow's excitement concerned James as he watched him run to the line; he wasn't about to let him go alone. He leapt from the parked car with Daniel and Samuel fast behind him.

The four boys stood silently in the line that roared around them. Within minutes, multiple men were behind them. Solidarity bonded them immediately—without even knowing if they would meet again.

The noise grew as more men lined up behind them. While the others only looked forward toward the doctors, tests, and the future, James examined the crowd. He listened to every comment he could pull from the endless roar. He laughed when one man claimed he wasn't telling his wife until a few days before he left because she would kill him before any German would. A total lack of respect for human life dripped from one man's lips as he exaggerated his joy in "killing them all," and James' disgust grew.

But the rest of the crowd, like James, was expectant for the next steps. After an hour of waiting, James watched his youngest brother walk into his physical assessment alone. He felt, in that moment, that his eighteen-year-old, little rat of a brother might finally be a man. Shortly after, James was ushered into a small room.

The room was clean but obviously used. At least one hundred men had likely been in the room before him. God only knew how many would come after. A short, exhausted doctor strode in from the door on the opposite side of the room.

"Name?" he said sternly.

"Dr. James Robert Harlow, sir," he answered. The doctor sized him up, looking first at his outward appearance and instructed him through a series of tests. His intelligence was tested through a list of seemingly meaningless questions that definitely were not a good judge of his intellect. Then came the eye exam. The doctor tested each eye, as if having a single good one was enough.

"Undress," the doctor ordered. James was no stranger to the human body, but as the person usually performing the examination, he felt extremely out of place. The doctor surveyed every last part of him—from his joints to his weight to his teeth.

All of this just to become a soldier, he thought. *At least it will be worth it in the end.*

"Get dressed." His thoughts were interrupted with the new instruction. James began to exit, ready to take his oath and receive his orders, when the doctor stopped him.

"I'm afraid I have some questions for you."

"Yes, sir," James answered, unsure of what questions the doctor could possibly have after the intricate examination.

"Do you typically have cold hands and feet?"

"Yes, sometimes," he answered slowly, confused about how the temperature of his feet would make a bit of difference. He watched the doctor scribble on the papers he held.

"Do you often feel fatigued throughout the day?"

"I suppose so. But as a doctor myself, I work long and irregular hours. I'm sorry, what is this about?" he asked, wondering why the questions seemed so specific.

"Please, Dr. Harlow, just one more thing." His hand reached for the stethoscope that James himself used countless times. Whatever the doctor was listening to—his heart or his lungs—James was now thoroughly concerned. The doctor removed his stethoscope from James' chest and looked at the floor.

"Dr. Harlow, it is my assessment you have anemia. I suspect it to be simply iron-deficient anemia, seeing as you have no more serious symptoms to suggest otherwise. But with the chill in your hands and feet, your fatigue, and your irregularly fast heartbeat, I'm afraid this will exclude you from the ability to participate in active service."

James' mind stilled. He marveled at his own inability to assess himself. He had seen the symptoms before—treated them even. But somehow, he had ignored his own health in the process of caring for everyone else's. His ears heard each word, but he failed to understand how this meant he would never go to battle with his brothers.

"Dr. Harlow? Dr. Harlow, did you hear me?"

The question made him jump. "No, I'm sorry. What did you say?"

"I said although you are unfit for active service, many hospitals in London would welcome a doctor of your expertise—specifically in surgery. I suggest you look into those to do your duty in a different manner."

"Yes, thank you. Is that all?" James was in no position to consider the logistics of his duty now the word *unfit* rang in his ears. The doctor nodded and James exited the room in a daze.

He followed the path of men smiling at the promise their examinations held, and his feet carried him back to the car. He slid down the side of the vehicle until he hit the ground where he lit a cigarette and took two deep puffs. He sat with his head back, looking up at the morning and feeling more useless than ever.

"James!" Daniel's voice rang out, and his heart sank into his stomach. He would have to listen to his brother's joy and share his own disappointment. He looked up at his brother, who stood over him, grinning, with Samuel and John beside him.

"Where were you? We looked for you after we took our oaths."

James looked up at Samuel forlornly. He knew each one had taken the oath; each one of them was able to serve. Each one would go to war—except him.

"My examination took longer than I anticipated," he answered, opening the car door and climbing in. The three soldiers looked at him, waiting for some kind of clue as to what he meant, then followed him into the car. The ride back to the Harlow estate was full of talk of training and when they would all be sent overseas.

"I wonder how long training will take," John said, smiling.

"Can't know for sure. But I do wonder where they'll send us after," Daniel answered.

"You boys sure you're ready for training? When's the last time you even broke a sweat? Pushing a pretty girl around a dance floor?" Samuel teased.

John and Daniel laughed and shoved him so hard the car shook. James stayed silent, letting them all think he too had taken the oath. He had not yet accepted himself that he would not be going with them.

"James, what's happened to you? You look white as a ghost," John teased.

James almost laughed at the irony of his brother listing yet another symptom of anemia.

"I have anemia," he started. "It's not dangerous. In fact, I've probably had it all my life. But it means I can't go with you. I was declined for active service." He spoke factually—delivering the diagnosis with no emotion like he had for so many families before, but never his own. He quickly shared the symptoms of anemia and how they matched the symptoms the doctor had identified, wanting the moment to pass. The car finally pulled to the front of the Harlow estate, and James was the first to exit—wanting to escape the pitiful stares he was receiving.

He met Lillian at the front door and wondered if she had even moved from her spot. She was standing in the exact same place she had been when they left. What had only been a few hours felt like days after the news James received. He could hear the others following him toward the house, but he never once turned around. He kept walking to Lillian. Her eyes asked a million questions, but instead he paused and squeezed her hand.

"They'll tell you. We'll talk later," he said, and he staggered into the house looking for his father's best scotch.

He found it in the dining room—where his father was undoubtedly drinking it the night before. He poured a fuller glass than he ever had before and took two long gulps. Lillian followed him into the room, and he watched, amazed, as she took the glass out of his hand and finished it off.

"Don't tell," she said with a smirk.

"They told you." He wasn't asking.

"John told me. Well, he told me you wouldn't go with them and said he'd kill enough for both of you." She laughed.

"Dumb boy. He must think they're going on holiday." James shook his head. He filled the gaps in John's retelling, and Lillian's face turned the same shade of pity he had seen in his brothers' eyes.

"I'm sorry, James. I am. But I won't pretend to be sad you'll be here."

"I won't be. I'm calling the doctor—the one that examined me. He offered me a job. I'm going to London. Somewhere between the drive back and this scotch, I decided I can't do nothing—not with the rest of them going. I can't just sit here, Lillian. If I can't go with them, I can at least do the thing I do best," he said—feeling every word deeply and knowing them to be true. He stepped around Lillian and followed the foyer back out to the car, his brothers, and Samuel. He looked at the trio and Lillian as she stood in the doorway.

He hugged Daniel and found himself envying him more than ever, nodded to John, hoping he would mature before the war forced it upon him, and shook Samuel's hand. Lillian emerged from the doorway and stood beside him. He turned to her—embracing his sister and hoping the war would not change her.

"You could tell him, you know," he whispered as he turned away toward his car.

As he looked out the window at his family, Lillian's glare faded to a smile. The boys simply waved.

"I hope not to see you boys until the war is over—make sure I don't," he yelled as the car jolted to life. The boys smiled, and James smiled back with a nod as the car carried him closer to London and to his own war.

CHAPTER 6

Samuel finished his work in a fog. His mind raced with sad thoughts of James' inability to serve in the army and his guilt and joy about his own enlistment. When his thoughts were not clouded in feeling sorry for James or dreaming of glory, his mind turned to his discussion with Lillian. She had been filled with anger and hurt he had not seen since they were children, and her mother told her she had to begin her formal lessons to become the perfect debutante. That kind of frustration had never once been directed toward him, and he hated it now sat on his shoulders.

His walk home haunted him, reminding him of the walk he had taken in the opposite direction to bring word of his father's death. Even though he felt secure in his decision to enlist—and most men would certainly follow—he knew what leaving his family meant. They were losing the only man they had left.

His steps carried him all the way to his small home. All at once, he saw a million things he had been meaning to fix. His mother asked him to paint the front door and mend the leaky windowpane that always seemed to let a constant stream into the house. These tasks were just the beginning of the list that flooded Samuel's mind as he entered. Suddenly, he wondered if he would ever get to them.

He entered and was immediately met by the warm glow that surrounded his home. He was constantly surprised his mother filled their humble little unassuming home with warmth so easily after the death of his father. Samuel took off his work shoes at the front door. They were covered in mud—from the Harlow grounds and from his trudge home. His mother had water on the stove for tea, but that was far from extraordinary. Whether it was their British heritage or simply his mother's desire to nurture, Samuel appreciated the knowledge that this conversation came with tea.

"Mum? Nel?" Samuel stuck his head through every door in the house, trying to find his ladies, but saw no one. He knew where they would be. Green thumbs ran in the family. So Samuel tugged back on his boots once more and followed his instinct around to the tiny plot of land behind their home his father had cherished. The little family was going to make sure his buds thrived in his absence.

Samuel found the pair of them right where he knew they would be. He gazed at his mother tending the land gently and his sister frolicking in her wildflower state. He stood and watched them silently. He wanted to remember them this way. He didn't want to spoil their day yet.

Anna Perry jumped when she finally saw him standing there. "Heavens! Samuel, you scared the daylights out of me. Get over here and help us."

But Samuel did not move. When he failed to follow his mother's instructions, her eyes swung back up to him. Samuel stood straight and tall—slowly becoming the soldier he had committed to be not yet twelve hours before. His mother stood slowly and walked toward her son as if she knew the words that were coming. She touched his arm as she passed him and returned to the house.

Now Samuel only faced his sister. Nellie had broken from her daydream state and met her brother's eyes. The pair watched their mother step over the threshold of their home. Instinctively, Nellie followed their mother's lead and grasped Samuel's arm. Together, they followed—staggering inside. Samuel took in the scene his mother had laid before them. She sat at the table with her cup of tea, bookended by two more cups at her children's places. No words were necessary, and both Samuel and Nellie sat quietly beside their mother.

"Tell me." Samuel's mother spoke quietly but firmly. She looked down at the small cup in her hands, only raising her head when Samuel finally spoke.

"I went to enlist today. Daniel, James, John and I all went to the recruiting office this morning." As Samuel spoke James' name, his sister's head snapped up in fear. He knew what her feelings would be, but he simply shook his head and continued. "Daniel came last night to tell them about the war, but he found me outside and told me first. I promised to go with them, and I did."

"You didn't think to tell your own mother before you left? You didn't think to inform me you intended to follow those boys to war?"

"I'm not following anyone. I made this choice myself. I wouldn't be satisfied staying here knowing other men are fighting."

"You mean dying."

His mother's words stung, but mainly because he had not thought of them. He had considered the honor, the glory, the excitement, and even what leaving his family would mean, but he had not yet thought about what his death would mean.

"I'm sorry, but I've made my decision. This is what I feel I need to do. I couldn't stay here while others went to fight, and you know that. I had my physical examination. I took my oath. I report for training in two weeks." It was one of the only times he could remember openly defying his mother and her wishes. He knew they only came from fear, but duty clung to him and demanded he choose this.

"Very well. If that's what you've decided," Anna Perry relented, staring at her son.

Samuel shrank under the weight of her eyes, and he knew she was only trying to make peace. He shrank further until his mother rose to kiss him and returned to the garden alone.

"She's proud, you know." Nellie's voice broke the silence. "She is. She's just scared. We both are, but he would be proud of you too."

Samuel nodded at her as she turned to follow her mother back out to the garden. He was left alone in his childhood home, feeling nostalgic for every brick and piece of furniture. He choked down the last drops of his tea and wandered to his bed. His little room didn't hold much—a few blankets, a picture of his father with Samuel's eyes and blonde hair, a handful of books Lillian had given him for birthdays or Christmas throughout the years, and a small mirror he shaved in front of most mornings. But even in its simplicity—Samuel saw his world. He saw his family's life, his friendship with the Harlow children, his father's death, his acceptance of his father's post, and his enlistment. The little room held so much of him in its cracks. He sat on the edge of his bed and put his head in his hands. Thoughts of his father swarmed.

Samuel's mind shifted to the Harlow boys. They would go to war together, and even if they were in different countries, fighting different battles—internal as much as external—at least they'd be together somehow. The thoughts kept coming until they consumed him completely and he was asleep.

* * *

The next morning, Samuel followed his usual path to work like any other day, but he felt different. He stood a little straighter, but the weight on his shoulders was a little heavier. He knew his walk would end with a conversation with Frederick Harlow—informing him of his choice to leave. Of course, his job might not be secure when he came back—if he came back.

He reached the Harlow estate in record time and walked straight to the front door where Mr. Taylor stood, greeting Samuel and the day together. Samuel had taken in every step of his walk and every moment he once took for granted. He took note of Mr. Taylor's steadfast presence.

"Good morning, Mr. Taylor. Is Mr. Harlow—"

"He's in the library, Samuel. He's been waiting for you." Mr. Taylor looked solemn, as always, but also worried. He seemed to know what the conversation in the library would entail.

Samuel walked through the front door like he had so many times and into the library. Frederick Harlow sat behind his large oak desk, waiting for Samuel.

"Samuel, I suppose I know what this is about." Mr. Harlow spoke without question, and it made Samuel wonder if the boys or Lillian had gotten to him first. The confusion on his face must have been clear, as Mr. Harlow continued. "John couldn't contain himself."

The pair smiled—laughing at the truth in it.

"I would have told you yesterday, but I hadn't yet told my mother or Nellie. I felt they deserved to know first."

"Of course, of course. We're proud of you, Samuel." Mr. Harlow emerged from behind the desk and extended his hand for Samuel to shake.

“Thank you, sir. I plan on working until I’m told to leave for training. Of course, that will only be a few weeks, but I’ll make sure everything is in order before I leave.”

Mr. Harlow nodded—clearly unsure of what to say next. But he led Samuel to the door and shook his hand once more.

“You are serving your country, and that’s something to be proud of. I hope you are.”

“Thank you, sir.” And he left.

He walked out of the library toward the front door. Before exiting the foyer, he turned to find Lillian on her usual perch at the top of the stairs. Their silence spoke more volumes than encyclopedias. Lillian’s mouth moved, but no sentence would fill the silence well enough. Samuel looked up at her, wondering what to say to reconcile after the words they had both spoken the day before. But he remained silent as well. Each yearned for some syllabic solitude from the other, but instead, Samuel smiled at his friend and turned to leave—heading toward the greenhouse.

His steps were small but focused as he progressed in his work. The greenhouse was his haven. As he stood in it happily daydreaming, the war, his fight with Lillian, and his responsibilities disappeared for a moment.

“You don’t need my permission.” Lillian’s voice came from behind him.

He turned to face her, wondering why, for the first time in her life, she sounded like she was apologizing first.

“What?” he asked, unsure of what she truly meant. She stepped toward him. Her sky-blue dress caught the soil that fell from the pots, but she didn’t seem to notice.

“You don’t need my permission,” she repeated. “But I’d like to give you my blessing—to go.”

Her words felt even more demeaning than permission would have, but Samuel simply nodded and accepted the sentiment. "Thank you, Lily. I wouldn't want to leave while you're angry with me. I couldn't."

"Oh, I'm still angry with you. I just don't want to be." She almost laughed but stopped it with her smile.

Samuel hung his head but kept his eyes on her. He flashed her the grin that always made her smile when they were young, and her stubborn look crumbled quickly.

"Don't be mad, Lil. I have to go. You know I do. I couldn't let your brothers go alone. I would leave eventually, if not now."

"I know. I just wish every man didn't have the desire to be a hero. Then at least one of you would stay."

He wondered how he could have missed it. The anger Lillian felt matched his mother's in so many ways—anger that dripped with fear and feelings of abandonment.

"We'll come back, Lillian."

Her full name made her turn back to meet his eyes. He only ever used it when the moment demanded sincerity. She stepped toward him but hesitated and folded her hands as if she was holding something she caught. Had she stifled another embrace?

He filled the gap himself and, standing inches from her, said quietly, "I'll come back."

He looked down at Lillian and waited for her reply, but instead, she took a slow breath in and stepped away from him. Before she left the greenhouse, she spoke with her back to him.

"You can't know that, but thank you."

"For what?"

"For trying to promise me you will."

And Samuel stood alone among the greenery.

CHAPTER 7

Samuel kept his word and worked until his orders came to report for training. But it came faster than he had expected. He had only one week to prepare, say his goodbyes, and report with Daniel and John. They had been granted the luxury of going to their training together, but after that, they would most likely be separated and scattered. John had been perpetually aggravated at the news the British army was holding soldiers younger than nineteen in training before they could be sent to the front.

"They can't let me join in the fun, can they? I enlisted and took the bloody oath!"

His rants would last hours, and Samuel would be forced to listen. But his frustration always made Samuel laugh. He secretly hoped the war would end quickly so John could avoid going anywhere but training. Of course, he would never admit it to the youngest Harlow.

Samuel's final day of employment at the Harlow estate began like every other—with the simple walk that had become his favorite companion. Each step welcomed him and waved goodbye simultaneously. He arrived at the greenhouse—the greenhouse that felt so much like his oasis rather than a manmade structure. He admired the handiwork he had inherited from his father—every bud, every piece of greenery. He roamed through the extensive hot rooms and stood in each one, staring up at the windowed ceilings and admiring the sun shining through each pane.

Mr. Taylor broke his trance when he entered with a small silver tray that contained a single letter.

"A letter for you, Samuel—or should I say Private Perry?" Mr. Taylor grinned.

"Thank you, Mr. Taylor. Thank you for always being so kind." Samuel smiled at the old Harlow butler, took the letter, and watched him leave with the tray. How strange he felt to be saying goodbye to his life's central figures like the walk and the butler. He looked at the letter, wondering who could have sent it.

He half smiled when he recognized Lillian's handwriting. Tearing it open, he chuckled again at the contents.

Dear Samuel,

Starting tomorrow, I will have to write you a letter instead of walking the grounds to find you. So today, I sent your first letter to the greenhouse. Meet me at the hill before going home today.

Your friend,
Lily

He smiled and tucked the small envelope in his back pocket, where it sat until his work was completed. After doing the last of his planting and preparing the ground for winter in a few short months, he put his tools away for the last time. He placed everything back in the glasshouse next to the empty pots, which waited for their new inhabitants next spring. Samuel only took his father's worn pair of gloves. He pushed the pair into his pocket where it met Lillian's letter. He pulled out the envelope and carried it in his hand until he reached the top of the hill.

Lillian sat on the ground in a white dress that cascaded over her legs and met the grass, which stained the hem. Her parasol sat beside her. Samuel knew she only brought it out of habit. The sun was setting directly ahead as he walked up behind her. He sat beside her, grazing her shoulder purposely with his, but he would claim it was accidental. He watched her staring at their favorite part of the Harlow land in silence.

"You requested my presence?" he teased.

She smiled and turned to face him.

"I wanted one more day on the hill," she said. "I wanted to give you your going-away present." He took in her smile—trying to remember every part of her face. He couldn't be sure when he would see it next.

From under the folded parasol, Lillian revealed a small package wrapped in paper. He smiled and took the parcel from her hands. He tore the paper away to find a small wooden box. It wasn't decorative or ornate, but the wood was stunning and glowed a caramel color in the fading sunlight.

Samuel lifted the lid to find a stack of papers wrapped in one of Lillian's pink hair ribbons. The parcel contained envelopes he was sure Lillian intended for him to send home, one picture of the entire Harlow family, and a stack of book pages clearly torn from their homes. As he examined them, he realized each one came from a different book—the ones they had stolen together. She'd demolished them for his sake. Samuel shook his head, but the sentiment warmed him to his core.

"Are these all of them?"

She smiled. "Well, not all of them—I had to leave father's library with a few whole books. But all the important ones are present and accounted for." As she spoke, her joy at the impact of her gift spread across her face.

Samuel thumbed through the pages—through the moments of their youth.

Each one held a story, a moment in time they had spent on the same hill. She had taken moments from each story and given them back to him as a grown man off to war. *Emma*—their first day together, *The Awakening*—their first moment of adulthood together, and every moment in between. His memories bled from *The Wizard of Oz* and *Sherlock Holmes and the Hound of the Baskervilles* to *Pride and Prejudice* and *Dracula*. Samuel folded them carefully with the envelopes and the photograph and put everything back into the box.

"Thank you so much, Lily. For everything." He spoke quietly—looking at the box in his lap, although he could feel her gaze on him. He stood slowly, then helped Lillian to her feet as well by offering his hands as a feeble excuse to touch hers.

"I suppose I should let you go home. Your mother will never forgive me if I steal you away on your last night."

Samuel smiled and slipped his hand from hers. "Goodbye, Lily." He turned toward home and walked away from Lillian. How long would it be until he could say hello again?

"If you forget to write me, I'll join the Germans and kill you myself," Lillian called with an audible smirk.

Without turning, Samuel answered, "I look forward to it." And his smile carried him all the way home.

* * *

The sun had set completely by the time Samuel made it home. His mother stood in the doorway, tapping her wooden spoon on the door frame like she used to when she would call him home. He walked toward her, grinning like a boy in trouble. Whether from the death of his father or his enlistment, his mother's hair had lightened with scattered gray, and the wrinkles that framed her eyes had become more pronounced. Her frailty made it easy for him to scoop her up until her feet left the floor.

"I know the Harlows mean well by keeping you working until the last day, but I'd like to see my son before he goes to war." She laughed, returning to her previous demeanor. Her irritation was evident but clearly forced. It broke when another chuckle escaped her mouth. Soon Samuel's deep laugh joined hers. Their laughter followed them over the threshold and rang through the quiet house.

Inside, Samuel froze, stunned by the scene before him. Paper decorations had been hung throughout the house, and Nellie stood in the small kitchen with a feast of a cake in her hands. He smiled and reached for his mother's embrace once more.

"Thank you, Mum," he said.

"Well, don't get all weepy. Dinner isn't anything special, but your sister insisted on a cake and some decorations. She thought you needed something special for your last night home."

His sister put her masterpiece on the little worn table and crossed the room to him. She jumped into his arms like she did when they were younger.

The night continued exactly as it always did, but with the finality of the end of an era. Samuel wished to hold the moment forever—complete in its warmth. Nellie's baking skills made the cake taste more like the dirt he worked with during the day, but he ate every bite with a smile.

"Go finish packing, Samuel. I pulled out your father's old case for you. It's in your room with some things I cleaned for you." He laughed at his mother's inability to refrain from nurturing. Even though he was sure she still disapproved of his decision to enlist—her mothering had taken over.

Samuel walked to his room to find his father's well-loved case they had brought with them eleven years prior. He felt so strange knowing it now belonged to him. He looked over at his bed to find a huge stack of shirts and pairs of trousers folded neatly on top of his sheets. He shook his head, smiling.

A few things, he thought. *She washed everything I own.*

He packed the case with the box from Lillian stuffed in the middle of his shirts for safekeeping. Looking around the room, he marveled at how its emptiness made it look even smaller. He moved to put his case by the tiny table but paused when he heard the conversation coming from the kitchen.

"It would just be London, Mum. I wouldn't be anywhere dangerous." Nellie spoke like she was grown and sure. Samuel listened to the persistence in his sister's voice and wondered what would send her to London so eagerly.

"I'm not losing both of you. Your brother is hard enough to part with. I won't send you to be subjected to all the gore he'll encounter and possibly even more. You're not ready, and you're not going." His mother spoke more abruptly to Nellie than she had ever spoken to him about his enlistment. He listened for more, but his mother's footsteps moved closer to his own door until it opened.

"Do you have everything you need?" she asked sternly—clearly still boiling from her conversation with Nellie.

Samuel nodded, unsure if she was aware he had heard.

"I have everything, Mum. I'm all packed. I'm ready." Each word he spoke was an attempt to calm her, but he knew nothing he could say would completely reassure her. She lifted both hands to cup his face like she had when he was young and kissed his forehead. She attempted to hide the tears in her eyes, but choked on the words she spoke.

"Just because I don't want to lose you does not make me any less proud of you, my boy." Samuel accepted the hug his mother gave him, then she left his room. He watched her enter her own and close the door. She would likely not open it again until the next morning.

Samuel picked up his father's case once again and proceeded to the kitchen, where he found Nellie at the table. He set the case down, then joined his sister.

"London?" he asked.

Nellie looked up at him slowly and nodded. "I asked Mum if she would support me going to London to be a nurse. I want to be useful. The longer I thought of being here alone without you while so many go to fight—I wanted to do something more. I'm not the silly little girl I was, Sam. I want to do something important—like you."

Samuel smiled proudly. He had noticed his sister's growth weeks earlier, but in that moment, he knew she saw it herself.

"If you want to help, to do something important, you'll find a way. Write to me when you decide—tell me where you are." He smiled, knowing she would, and rose to return to his room.

"I love you, you know," she said quietly. Samuel turned toward her and nodded. He closed the door to his room and laid down. The uncertainty of the next weeks and months loomed over him until he finally drifted off to sleep, waiting for the morning.

CHAPTER 8

Samuel woke with a start as Nellie burst into the room and flung open his curtains so the fresh morning sunlight demanded a place in his room. His eyes had been open for hours, but the new light made him shut them suddenly—feeling the sting of the day. Nellie walked to his bedside and stood over him, teasing.

"Sam, you know soldiers are supposed to be punctual and prepared, right?"

Samuel had lain in his bed until the last possible moment. He rose slowly, and went to his tiny mirror, and swiped the small safety razor across his face until it was smooth again. He went to the end of his bed where his mother had laid his only suit—his funeral suit. He felt out of place wearing anything nice on the way to training, but his mother would never allow him to go to the train station not looking his best—even when she did not approve of his destination. He pulled on his trousers and drew his suspenders over his shoulders. He let the jacket drape over his arm, unsure if he would even put it on as he walked out to the kitchen. The August heat poured in from the windows and made the little home burn from the inside-out. Sweat formed on Samuel's neck down his only unpacked shirt.

He exited his room, expecting to find the whole family, but saw only Nellie. She stood in the kitchen, still in her nightgown, and smiled at him. She must have noticed the confusion on his face, as she answered the unasked question.

"She left early to go to the market. She said she told you goodbye last night after you finished packing. But truly, I don't think she could bear it." Each word she spoke echoed an apology.

Samuel nodded. His sadness bled into understanding slowly. His mother had come as close as she could to accepting his choice the night before and was undoubtedly trying to part with him in the best way she could manage.

"Do what you feel is right, Nel—about London. She won't like it if you go, but if you feel like it's right—do it. You'll make the right choice. Your heart is the biggest I've known." He pulled his sister into an embrace, and they stood in the middle of their home, silent and still. He reluctantly let her go when the moment had passed, and he knew it was time to go.

"I'm proud of you, Sam. Write to us when you can." Tears formed in her eyes, but she smiled. Samuel watched her and took in the final melancholy moments of the morning in his home. He hugged her once more and kissed the top of her head.

"I love you."

And he was gone.

He walked out the door, shutting it behind him and leaving his sister inside alone. Each step away from the Harlow estate made him feel as if he was truly walking into an unknown world. His first trip away from home was to become a soldier.

The station was a large brick building Samuel had only been to a few times in his life. Once, had been the week before to buy his ticket. He walked into the building to check the timetable and followed the flow of young men undoubtedly all going to the same place he was. He stood on the platform outside, waiting for the train, certain of his decision—until he saw her.

Lillian.

She stood in a soft pink dress that draped over her shoulders and fell just above her feet. She wore a hat Samuel knew was one of her favorites—the front dipped just below her right eye and the back was covered in silvery-white feathers. She carried the parasol from the night before in her gloved hands and held it so tightly he could see the redness of them through the thin fabric. She looked so put together Samuel wondered which maid she had bribed to help her dress so early in the morning. He walked toward her carefully—not knowing what to expect.

"Lily, what are you doing here? Is something wrong?" With their goodbyes said the day before, something must have happened to lead her to the station on the morning of his departure.

"Nothing's wrong. Everything is fine."

Samuel breathed a sigh of relief but still couldn't understand why she had come. He feared the answer, but he asked the question once more. "Why are you here?"

She looked at him from under the brim of her hat and spoke loudly to be heard over the whistle that blared as the train pulled into the station. "I have to tell you. I have to say it, and we can't know if you'll come back, so it has to be now."

He dropped the case beside him and stepped back, knowing exactly what she meant. He had never allowed himself to imagine a moment like the one Lillian had just created.

He knew it wasn't possible—and it killed him before he even reached a battlefield.

"Don't do this, Lillian. Not now, not today. It's not true." His eyes met hers and attempted to apologize without speaking. The words he wished they could have spoken a thousand times before, he now tried to still before either of them felt their impact.

"What do you mean it's not true?"

"We're all leaving. Daniel, John, and I to training. James to London. You're scared of being here alone. You've never been alone. You've always had me or your brothers or a thousand men lurking around you. You're holding on to our childhood, not to me."

He watched her step back as he had, clearly offended by his words.

"Yes, I resent the four of you for leaving me. But that's not what this is. That's not why I'm here. That's not all of it. You know it isn't."

He shook his head. He dreaded hearing these words. Refusing the feeling was easier when the words remained unsaid.

"You don't know what you're doing. You don't know what you're asking." He wanted with every shred of his soul to tell her she was right—to tell her he had tried to say the same thing so many times before. But he never could. He had no promise of employment when he returned—if he returned. This one moment could destroy his family's security if he let it.

"I know exactly what I'm asking," she said. "I know you. I know you think roses are a stuffy society flower, but no person alive can grow them like you can. I know you've walked home the same way ever since my father hired you because it's the path your father took. I know you got embarrassed reading all the love scenes in the books I brought you when we were young, but you read them aloud for me anyway. I know you know just as many seemingly insignificant details about me as I know about you. That's what I want. That's what I'm asking. I'm asking for a lifetime of knowing you."

Samuel stayed stiff as a board—his face blank and his feet unable to move toward her or walk away. So he stood stationary in the middle of the train platform and listened to the whistle wind down the time he had left in Staffordshire.

"Lillian, I can't. You would be ruined by me—cast out in every possible way. I would never have a job in your home again—your father would see to it. They might love me like a son, but make no mistake—I am not. And what you're asking would guarantee my dismissal. I'm the only one providing for my family apart from any mending my mother takes on from the town. I am what keeps us here, and my job with your family is what allows us to stay."

"You'll not even admit I might be right? That you've felt the same way since we were young—possibly even before I did?"

She saw him, and he knew it. All the cracks and crevices that held the most intimate parts of his heart—she saw them all.

"My place and your position always took precedence over our feelings. It has to do the same now."

Suddenly, the whistle blew once more, and Daniel and John appeared behind Lillian on the platform. He had not even considered she might have come with her brothers in the same car.

"Lillian, what are you still doing here?" John asked. She shook her head as her gloved hand reached up to brush away a single tear.

"She wanted one more goodbye, I suppose. Let's go." Samuel spoke for her, and his voice remained steady and unchanged even though the words felt like sandpaper in his mouth. Daniel and John walked away from the pair and handed their bags to the porter.

Lillian stared at him, but he could think of nothing to console her, change his mind, or mend what had just been broken.

"I won't tell them. You'll have your position when you get back." She backed away from him and turned back toward the sitting area inside the train station. She stopped when Daniel's voice rang out.

"Samuel, come on. Our car is here."

Samuel looked at Daniel and smiled. His gaze turned to Lillian, and she held it while he spoke. "Your car is there, Daniel. My ticket is not for first class. My place is here. I'll meet you when we arrive."

Lillian faced him fully now, and Samuel felt the weight of the words. He said them to Lillian as much as he said them to his companions. It wasn't news to him the Harlow children remained constantly unaware of his place and status. On the day that made most of them soldiers together, the day that leveled them, he felt the weight of his class most of all.

Samuel turned away and entered his car. He put his case on the seat beside him, separating himself from the family who sat near him. As the final whistle blew, he raised his head to see Lillian alone on the platform, watching him leave. Her gaze never faltered.

Samuel finally turned away as his car passed her, and he never once looked back.

CHAPTER 9

Lillian stood completely still on the platform for nearly ten minutes after the train had carried her brothers and Samuel away. Her moment of blind courage, her declaration, left her alone and feeling completely foolish. Part of her wished she had never done it and another wished she had done it long ago—perhaps it would have mattered then.

She loved him. And he left.

She walked in a daze to the car. Their family chauffeur opened the door. She slid in and sat quietly, barely hearing the driver when he asked if she had anywhere else to go. She shook her head slowly and felt the car jolt to a start. As the vehicle carried her from the station toward home, she finally understood the loss her heart suffered with Samuel's no. Tears poured, and she let them. She didn't once stop them like she had with the one that fell in front of the boys.

The car weaved through the streets until it passed the Perry place. Would it ever seem whole again after William's death and Samuel's departure? Lillian thought not.

"Stop the car."

The driver halted abruptly a few yards from the home, and Lillian stepped out. She walked to the little house and rapped at the door. Nellie emerged, and Lillian found herself in tears once again. Nellie ushered her inside, and Lillian managed to wave the driver on to her own home.

She hadn't been inside the Perry home since she was a child—before she and Samuel had both grown older, which made the visits seem less proper. To her delight, it hadn't changed. It still felt warm, and she was surprised it seemed more like a home than her own ever had. The Perry family managed to live in such close quarters, but Lillian felt strangled living in a different wing of her home than her mother. Their closeness didn't kill them the way her own family's did.

Nellie scurried around the kitchen, putting water in the kettle and carrying it to the stove to boil. Lillian stood in the middle of the little room looking at the intricacies of Samuel's life and felt the weight of his absence more than ever. Nellie gestured to the little chair next to the table as the whistle blew, and she set a small cup and teapot in front of Lillian. The littlest Perry was so much like Samuel. Their kindness was incomparable, and their ability to nurture flowed from them both so easily. Even though he was now miles away, Samuel's touch extended all the way back home to her.

"Lillian, what happened?" Nellie asked as she sat and poured her own cup of tea.

Lillian stripped her arms of the gloves that bound her hands and took a deep breath before raising the small white teacup to her mouth.

"I've just come from the train station." Nellie looked at her with a slight smile and waited for the next words. "I was telling the boys goodbye."

"Your brothers or all the boys?"

Lillian raised her head and lowered the cup. Her tears began again, but she choked them back and swallowed hard, wanting them to fade.

"I told him." She looked up at his sister, knowing Nellie would understand her words. "I told him and he refused it. All of it. John and Daniel interrupted, but it didn't matter. He wasn't going to change his mind. They're all gone."

Nellie lowered her cup slowly and looked at Lillian, waiting for more, but Lillian said nothing.

"I'm leaving too Lillian." Nellie's head dipped.

Lillian's head whipped up so quickly, she almost lost her hat.

"What do you mean, *leaving*?" Lillian's tone trembled.

"I won't be far—just London. I'll be with James at the hospital. I want to help, Lillian. I want to be a nurse." Nellie spoke quietly and quickly, as if the pain would lessen the faster she talked.

Lillian's eyes welled with tears once more, but this time they shone. Her own fears remained, but the small girl in front of her was becoming a woman. Her heart filled with pride as easily as it broke.

"I'm proud of you, Nellie. I'm happy to know you'll be with James. He'll look after you."

"Who will look after you, Lillian?"

Lillian smiled at the question. "I suppose I'll have to." The reality of her own words—the understanding that for the first time in her life she was alone with her parents and stuck—made her hope no bad news entered their home. "When do you leave?"

"I'm not sure. I'd like to leave as soon as possible, but Mum isn't happy with my decision. I might stay for a bit to make it easier for her." Nellie's smile faded as she spoke of her mother's disapproval. Lillian thought it must be the only time Mrs. Perry had ever disapproved of her daughter.

What must that feel like? she wondered. *To live not feeling like a mother's pride has to be earned?*

"She loves you, but you have to do what you think is right."

Nellie smiled at the comment, and Lillian sat confused at the obvious glee that spread across her friend's face.

"That's what Samuel said," Nellie explained.

At the mention of his name, Lillian took a deep breath and choked as she let it out.

"Funny, you two always seemed in step with each other—even when we all were young. I envied you two. I wanted someone to understand me the way you understood each other." Nellie continued, clearly reminiscing.

Lillian wished she wouldn't.

"Well, you must have misunderstood us." Lillian spat the words, tasting the sting of them in her mouth.

Nellie shook her head and smiled. "I don't think so. But he's a family man first. He feels responsible for us. Even if it means giving up what he's wanted most since our first day here."

Lillian forced a smile. Nellie used to follow her around as a little girl, and they had become so similar. She now yearned for Nellie's strength. Lillian rose slowly, and Nellie followed. Lillian pulled both gloves back on her hands and walked to the door. As she exited the little house, she looked back as Nellie stood at the threshold.

"Goodbye, Lillian."

"Goodbye, Nellie. I hope you go to London—even if it means missing you terribly. You'll be brilliant. Write to us, and make that brother of mine write too." She smiled one last time and began the walk home, following the impressions of Samuel's work boots that seemed permanently stamped in the ground.

As the day dragged on and the sun grew hotter, Lillian practically melted under the heat and tore off her hat and gloves. Every curl added to her hair that morning had evaporated. Before long, it had fallen completely, and only her dark natural curls remained. Her mother always stated they weren't enough to attract any man worth having. Lillian staggered up to the front door of the Harlow estate, disheveled and exhausted by the morning's events. Carrying her hat, gloves, and heart, she strode boldly through the front door.

"Miss Lillian," Mr. Taylor said. "Your parents were worried when the chauffeur returned without you from the Perry house. Your mother has been in a state all morning."

"She's always in a state over my choices, Taylor. Today is no different."

She walked through the foyer and up the stairs, which now felt so different without John's noise or Samuel's presence. Each step felt heavier than the last, but she finally made it to her bedroom. Her mother sat in the corner waiting for her. Mary Harlow lounged near the vanity and sighed loudly to make her irritation clear—as if it wasn't already.

"Lillian Katherine Harlow. Where have you been?"

Her mother's drama always initiated eye rolls from Lillian. She threw her sweat-drenched hat and gloves on the four-poster bed, which was done up with the same pastel pink as the dress she wore.

"I was out. I told you I was going to the station with Daniel and John."

"You could have said your goodbyes here. What was so crucial you had to follow them to the train?"

The only thing more invasive than her mother's opinions about her marriage prospects were her suspicions about Lillian's activities. Lillian wasn't sure Samuel had been correct about her parents' disapproval, but if either would find trouble with her friendship with Samuel, it would be her mother. It would be easier to say nothing.

"I wanted them to have someone from home at the station with them. It certainly wasn't going to be you. You did nothing but weep all morning." Lillian undressed down to her petticoat—shedding every moment of the day and wishing it gone from her skin.

"It's perfectly normal for a mother to grieve the departure of her sons." Her mother rose and made her way toward the door. "Did Samuel get away safely?"

Lillian remained at the side of the bed, grasping the column to steady herself.

Of all the ways she could have asked, she thought.

"Yes. Yes, he got away," she said.

She turned to see her mother nod and exit her room. Lillian slid her hand down the column and let the rest of her body follow until she sat on the floor, cursing the heat and her corset. She considered what the next months would bring—each day would be spent hoping to hear no news from the front and each man she loved would be safe.

She turned toward her bed and sat on her knees, praying like she had in the early morning the day war began. Each word was pulled from the deepest parts of her heart, and she begged safety for each of them. When she had finished, she forced herself to stand and pull on her robe. She walked to her vanity where her mother had been sitting and pulled paper from the lowest drawer. Without hesitation, she did the only thing she knew how.

She penned a letter to her friend. She wrote to Samuel.

My dear Samuel,

I've dreaded the day we would part since you first came to us when we were children. Do you remember that day? Mother had told us two new children would come to play with us. A boy named Samuel for Daniel, James, and John and a girl, Nellie, for me.

You arrived, and Nellie ran through the grounds with the boys to find flowers and any kind of creature wilder than they were. You asked me if we had any books. Our first moment of mischief together. You lifted me through the window so easily into my father's library, and I took the first book my hand touched. It was Emma. We raced to the hill that would become our spot and read of Emma Woodhouse and Mr. Knightley.

I saw so much of us in them even then. Emma was spunky and meddlesome and always thought her idea the best. Mr. Knightley was older, wiser, more sensible, and the most loyal of friends. I think I dreamt they were us. I dreamt we would become the good friends they were and, as time grew, that maybe one day we might risk everything for the sake of gaining each other.

Please forget what I told you when you left us. You were right, of course. It was nothing more than childhood dreams and a wish to not be left alone in this house with only my parents for company.

But look at you now, Sam. Today, you begin your journey—risking everything for our country. I do not know where they will send you. I do not know when I'll see you next. I do know

I'll pray for you often and think of you always. When you miss me—if you miss me—think of the little girl you snuck into the library, and make sure you get back to her.

Your friend,
Lily

CHAPTER 10

James had not slept for thirty-six hours, but he felt nothing. The longest shift he had taken was forty-two—almost two full days. British forces had only been on French soil for a few weeks, but with the number of bodies he had seen, one would think the war had already dragged on for years. The London hospital was well-lit but felt dingy with the soldiers lying side by side and begging for relief from the pain.

The last hour alone had brought James one leg amputation, two cases of dysentery, and one shrapnel extraction from a man's shoulder. His shift finally ended as he tore the last shred from the soldier's clavicle, and the man fell unconscious. James wiped the blood from his hands and walked away from the table.

"Nurse," he said to one of the nameless faces who followed him, waiting for orders. "Dress this man's wounds and change the bandages every six hours." He tore off his bloodied coverings, revealing the honorary uniform that consistently burned into his skin like a lie. His strides got increasingly longer as he reached for his case and headed for the front door of the hospital.

How strange, he thought. *Every man thought he'd leave this war whole, while so few do—even the ones with all their limbs.*

James' thoughts consumed him until he collided with a person walking up the steps—knocking them both to the ground. He caught sight of strawberry blonde hair and a dress that looked identical to one of his sister's. When the woman looked up at him, she cried out with laughter and attacked him with an embrace on the hospital steps.

"James!" Nellie giggled. "I can't believe I found you so quickly."

James laughed at her excitement, and her familiar face made his exhaustion almost bearable. He helped her to her feet and smiled. "Nellie, what are you doing here? Lillian didn't write to tell me to expect you."

"She didn't know what day I was coming. Neither did I until last night. I've been communicating with the head doctor—Dr. Walker. I've been taken on as a nurse here."

James was stunned but secretly pleased to have someone he knew serve with him.

"Dr. Walker is a good man. He's inside. I was just going home for the night, but I'll walk you inside and make sure you get settled in."

Nellie nodded and picked up the cases she had flung on the steps. Random shoes and garments had fallen down the front steps, which made James chuckle. He helped her scoop them up, and they walked back in the building. He turned in time to see the color empty from Nellie's face. He hadn't noticed the stench on himself since he had worked in it for so long, but he could imagine how it would strike someone new.

"I had no idea—"

"—what you signed up for?" James finished.

Nellie shook her head. "No, how bad it already was." He watched her look around at the nurses bustling and the men lying still. "We've only occupied France for a month, James. How is it already like this—so many beds already filled?"

James shook his head, looking for answers or a response to fall out of his mouth, but nothing did. He saw the look of determination spread across her face the same way it had for so many nurses before her. Only a fraction of them had been able to stay—to endure what they had seen. He wondered if Nellie would be capable, but he led her further into the hospital to Dr. Walker. He was a tall, lean man with a pointed nose and a lofty gaze that demanded respect he had yet to earn from James.

"Dr. Walker, this is—"

"Eleanor Perry. Nice to meet you—I'm Dr. Walker."

James was taken aback by the sound of Nellie's full name and scanned his brain. Had he ever heard it before? James turned once more to Nellie.

"I live just down the street, Nel. The other nurses know where if you need anything." He watched her smile fade once more—clearly stunned by the comment about the nurses. Wartime bred loneliness and frankness, and the faster Nellie's crush on him disappeared, the better. He wasn't blind to it—he never had been—but 1914 held no room for a little girl's frivolity.

He watched Nellie follow Dr. Walker slowly—raising her head and walking tall behind him as he showed her the rest of the old building. The pair disappeared up the dirtied staircase, and James retraced his steps to exit the hospital.

James walked back down the street to his flat and felt every moment of the day rise from his shoulders and fall. Knowing tomorrow would bring similar weariness could send him through the pavement. He keyed into his room that held very little: a stove that had never been turned on, a bed that was not slept in often enough, and a small desk where he kept his letters and his whiskey.

If my mother heard what I told Nellie, or if she could see the state of this room, she'd faint, he thought and smirked. *Oh, the simple pleasures of being the disappointing son.*

He poured himself some whiskey and gulped hard and fast—finishing the glass faster than he ever had. He threw his hat and jacket over the back of the chair, letting the rest of his clothes land wherever they fell, and staggered to the bathroom. He filled the tub with water, slid into it, and let the top of the water splash over the edges and cover the floor surrounding it. He sat in silence until the water was cold and filled with the stains of his day. He could only remain in it a few moments after the warmth had faded before rousing himself. The longer he sat, the nearer to sleep he crept. He dried himself and moved to the bed in the last pair of underpants he had from home. He thought about the times he didn't appreciate when his dirty things would disappear and be replaced with clean.

He sat half naked in the rickety little chair he had borrowed from the abandoned room next door. There were new, unopened letters on his desk, and he sighed. The building manager had once again entered his room without permission rather than sliding his mail under the door. But he soon forgot his distaste for the nosy busybody when he saw the handwriting of one of the letters.

Samuel.

He knew Samuel was fresh out of training and must be in the trenches by now. He tore open the letter himself, not even bothering with the letter opener that lay beside him, and read the contents slowly and carefully—taking in every word.

Dear James,

I'm safe. At least right now. I know that's what you'll worry about the moment you see a letter from me. For right now, I'm fine. I've been sent to France with Daniel, but we're stationed miles apart. I hope to see him again under better circumstances. John remains in England waiting impatiently to be sent abroad. The military is wary of sending anyone under the age of nineteen overseas, as I'm sure you know. Unfortunately, he won't have long to wait, since his birthday is in November. I hoped this would all be over by then so he would be one less person to worry about.

How is the hospital? I pray daily you get less men than the day before, but I'm afraid that may be in vain. I see so many bodies myself.

Has Nellie arrived? She wrote me she would be going soon. I know she's young, but she seems determined to serve in London. Look out for her. She's capable, but she's still my sister. Make sure she doesn't come anywhere near here—even if they tell her they need more nurses, even if they send you here for field surgeries, don't let her come. I'm sure she's seeing enough horror for one lifetime in London alone.

Praying for you often and hoping to see you sooner rather than later with the war behind us.

Your friend,
Samuel

James smiled at the letter—happy for any news from Samuel and his brothers. But the smile faded as he wondered how many more letters he would receive before the war was truly over—just over a month already felt too long. The next letter under Samuel's came in a flowing, familiar script only his sister could write.

Those two, he thought. *Always together, even in wartime.* He slid his thumb under the blazing red seal stamped with an *L* and began reading once more.

My dearest brother,

I told him. Just like you said I could, but don't expect this letter to be full of joy, because the opposite is far closer to the truth. Samuel could not return the feelings I hold for him. In truth, I'm not sure I ever said the words out loud, but the sentiment was rejected for the sake of his future occupation and, I'm assuming, my status. Maybe he's right. There's a reason I've hidden everything from our parents this long, and there's a reason I sighed with relief when you told me you were the only one who had seen that day at the graveyard. Perhaps I knew what his answer would be. Perhaps I knew what our parents would say. Either way, I hope our friendship remains, but in his eyes, that is all that can ever exist.

Nellie must be there now. I let her borrow my dress to come in—she needed something nice, and I wanted to do something small for her. Doesn't she look so grown in it? How we've all grown since the Perrys came to us. I hope you'll look after her—and yourself, of course. I pray for you often. Please return the favor, as I remain at home with our mother. She is frantic daily over you and dreams of marrying me off to a man in uniform.

As if that could somehow make a dull man more tolerable. We shall see, I suppose. Write to us more often.

All my love,
Lillian

James smiled once more at his sister's jokes about their mother's eccentric nature, but he felt Lillian's pain over Samuel's rejection.

That stupid boy.

His mind finally turned to sleep, but before it could move him completely to the bed, he answered his sister. Even though it took all his might to hold the pen upright, he sealed the letter and placed it on the desk to take with him when a knock would inevitably come in a few hours to call him back to the hospital. He poured himself one more glass of whiskey and downed it before falling into his bed and into one of the deepest slumbers of his adult life.

CHAPTER 11

Samuel had been in France for only two weeks, but he had already developed a distaste for the country and wished never to return. The inside of his trench was his only sight from morning until night. Unlike the ground he'd loved and tended at the Harlow estate, which brought life and beauty, the dusty brown walls of the trench brought only death, disease, and destruction.

He was stirred awake by something nibbling at his foot. It had already gnawed a hole in the fabric near his toes. His eyes came into focus to see a ragged little rat, clearly as hungry as he was, making a meal of his boots. He kicked the creature off and sat up, waiting for instructions. The sky was dark and the depth of the trench made the night even more shadowy. The walls extended only a little above Samuel's head while the bottom of the trench often filled with rainwater and vermin. The man who sat beside him greeted him with a nod.

"Anything new?" Samuel asked.

"Nothing, Private. We're still waitin' on the damn Germans to do something."

Samuel had never thought war would involve so much waiting. The rain of bullets was something he and the other soldiers both yearned for and hoped never came. The letters that came and went were some of the only shreds of light that dared shine into the pit Samuel found himself in. His helmet lay beside him—already covered in dirt and experience, and he pulled it on when he heard gunshots firing in the distance.

"Relax, soldier. We've still got time. Those were the patrols. They were sent out while you were sleeping."

The soldier beside him had become his companion over the last week, but Samuel had neglected to learn his name. He smirked at his oversight and extended his hand slowly with a smile. "Samuel Perry."

"Albert Blake." The soldier reached for his hand and shook it with a return nod. Albert reached inside his jacket and revealed two cigarettes.

Samuel had never smoked before the war, but it was another way to pass time. He took the cigarette and pulled matches from his boot, lighting his own and his new acquaintance's. The pair sat in silence, both obviously waiting for the other to speak or for the eventual shooting to begin.

"Where are you from, Albert?" Samuel finally asked.

"Surrey. You?" he asked, jabbing his cigarette toward Samuel.

"Staffordshire," he answered. Even the name sounded far away. His home existed both in another country and another time. His mind went to his mother, Nellie, and even to Lillian, who he had been trying to keep his mind off of. Albert must have seen the wheels turning behind Samuel's eyes, because the next question came quick.

"You got a girl back there? I've got one back home—waiting for me to marry. Said she'll not accept a proposal until we win the war. Stubborn little thing, but I love her." He pulled a picture from his jacket right beside his heart and handed it to Samuel. The picture showed a lovely girl with kind eyes and light hair. Samuel smiled and returned the photo, feeling the weight of its value.

"No, I don't have a girl. I guess I could have had one, but—" his words cut short when his mind failed to catch up. Did he not have a girl because of his own doing? Or because of the way of the world? He remained unsure. Either way, he didn't have her.

"That's alright," Albert started. "All girls like a man in uniform. You go back when we win this thing, and you'll find one soon enough."

He took his new friend's attempt at consolation and nodded gratefully. Whether the conversation was finished or not, neither spoke again. Instead, Samuel went back to his little patch of dirt where a blanket lay for him and covered the little box he kept protected at all costs. He pulled the contents from the box and stared at the portrait of the Harlow family, hoping for the safety of each one.

He returned the picture and reached for a piece of paper to begin a letter. He sat staring at the blank page for a few minutes in dead silence—his pen never once touching the page. He had begun so many letters to Lillian but burned each one to warm his hands instead of sending it. The letter he had received from her when he was still in training held words he had practically memorized. He wished more than anything he could respond to her, but no words seemed right or good enough. Finally, when he was ready to write something—anything, a voice startled him.

"Perry, mail," said a faceless soldier who threw a letter at him and was gone in a matter of seconds. Samuel reached for the small envelope and examined the writing he knew belonged to his sister. He ripped it open quickly, hoping for any and all news of home.

Dear Samuel,

I'm hoping and praying you are safe daily. London is busier than home but feels much the same somehow. I think after the war—whenever that may be—I could be happy here. I'm not sure any life before the war exists—for anyone.

Nursing men throughout this war is more frightening than I ever thought it would be. I've seen more discarded parts of men—arms and legs chopped off bodies—than full men in the few days I've been here. I know there will be even more to come. I feel this war is far from over.

James is here, which I would have taken comfort in at one point, but I fear he will return half the man he once was. As harrowing as my experience has been, he has done so many of the cuts, and I know he feels each one. How fast we've grown up. All of us.

Please write to me soon, but don't tell me everything. I'd rather not know how close you are to one of the beds I tend. I hope we will all be home at the Harlow estate soon, but until then—I love you dearly.

Your sister,
Nellie

PS. Lillian told me what happened when you left. Stop avoiding her. She asks for word of you often. Write the poor girl.

Samuel rolled his eyes at her postscript message. He knew she was right—he had to write her. But he would never tell

Nellie her meddling was correct. He folded the note and unwrapped the bundle of book pages to add it to the pile of treasure and secure it with Lillian's hair ribbon again. The soft and pink little scrap of fabric stood out so boldly in the pit he lived in. He held it for a moment and smelled the perfume that floated from it but quickly returned it to the box, hoping to save the small scent from home as long as he was able. Not knowing how much more waiting he could endure now that his cigarette was gone, he reached for the paper and tried to write once more.

* * *

Samuel woke again, but this time the sun woke with him. He raised his head to look at what the morning had brought but lowered it again—disappointed that only more waiting awaited him. He stood slowly and felt his socks rub raw against his feet under his tightly knotted boots. Albert Blake appeared from the end of the trench and shuffled toward him.

"Perry, let's go."

Samuel, still dazed from sleep, sat up and faced his new friend. "What? Go where?"

"We're going to clear the trench."

Samuel hung his head at the chore. At least it would occupy his time for the next handful of hours. Albert offered a hand and helped him to his feet.

The pair walked up and down the trenches collecting everything from cartridge cases to discarded socks. The other men littered the trenches much like their abandoned things. They looked forgotten and thrown to the sides, waiting for someone to move them—to tell them to do something, anything.

Samuel finally limped back to his small cot and collapsed on it. Samuel pulled off his left boot, removed the sock, and let his foot breathe. In training, Samuel and the other men had been warned about trench foot, but never did he think it would occur or cause the pain he now felt. Before Samuel could pull off the other boot, he looked up to see Albert standing over him.

"Perry, when's the last time you had your boots off?"

"I'm not sure—maybe three days."

Albert shook his head and removed Samuel's other boot and sock carefully. Samuel stared at his feet, which had a full layer of soggy skin covering the bottom. It was falling off in between his toes and sagged off the entire arch of his foot. He had never before felt so disgusted by one of his own ailments. Albert bent down and reached for a change of socks that laid on top of Samuel's cot.

"What are you doing?" Samuel asked, wincing as Albert slid them onto his feet.

"Well, clearly you were told about trench foot, but you were obviously not taught how to prevent it. Were you not given a partner when you arrived?"

"A partner?" Samuel's voice dripped with pain.

"When you arrive, you should be given a partner or pair yourself with someone to remind you to check your feet. Because, as you can see, we normally forget to do it ourselves. Wash your feet when you can. Make sure you dry them completely. Change your socks often. Take your boots off when you can, and stop tying them so tight, Perry. I'll be your partner, but I'm not putting socks on your feet again." Albert laughed, and Samuel cracked a smile at his new comrade.

"I'm not going to lose my feet, am I?" Samuel asked.

"Not if you do what you're bloody told," Albert yelled as he walked back down the trench toward his own cot.

Samuel wondered how he had neglected the one thing he needed the most when he returned—next to his hands. He was no good to his family dead, but he wasn't any better to them crippled. The rest of the day brought more waiting, two more sanitary walks with Albert supporting him and his healing feet, four more cigarettes smoked, and one sad excuse for a nap.

Albert came back to Samuel's station shortly after the sun went down. He sauntered up slowly with two more men—one on either side. One stood tall and lanky like a teenager, but his eyes held stories of twelve years Samuel had not yet lived. His mustache draped over his grin, which was missing a tooth or two.

"This is Christopher," Albert said, motioning to the man. Samuel was unsure if it was his first or last name but didn't bother asking.

The other man stood just as tall, but his broad shoulders and extra pounds extended him horizontally as well. He hunched his back—most likely from trying to protect his head from stray bullets—but his stride suggested he walked similarly without fearing a shot in his direction. He looked roughly Samuel's age but like he had lived a little more, and not in a good way.

"And I'm George Warding," he said, extending his hand.

Samuel greeted the men with a smile, but every new person he met and befriended made him wonder how long he would know them. He already hoped and prayed so often for the friends he could not see. He wasn't sure how he would manage if one of these new friends died in front of him. Even in the waiting—the mindless, quiet waiting—Samuel knew it was a possibility.

He let his thoughts roam free and instead just thanked the men for their company. George pulled a ratty deck of cards from his pocket, opened them, and dealt. Each card was dirty from the elements and the men's hands that touched them. Everyone was coming apart in places, but the men all took them willingly—happy for the distraction and any pastime that took away the monotony of their days.

Samuel laughed his way through losing each of the three games they played. Eventually, the men all stalled their cards and conversations stirred instead. The discussion almost instantly turned to home or what they would do when they got back. The latter conversation always ended quickly as each man felt the weight of the small word *if* hanging in the air beside them and making them all feel mortal. Samuel listened intently to each man's story—fascinated by lives so different than his own and also exactly the same.

"I'm going home to London when this hell is over," Christopher said, waving his hands. "I don't know what I'll do or who I'll do it with, but it's gotta be better than sitting here with you lot." His crass comments made each man chuckle. "Both my parents died before I was thirteen. I was working in a factory by sixteen. Thank God I didn't have nobody but me—I barely ate myself." He laughed at his own misfortune, but Samuel saw the weight of his life and understood the load his eyes held.

"I'm not sure where I'll go," George interjected. "I've never been anywhere else but England—I might not come to France again," he said with a chuckle, "but I think I want to get out." Samuel wondered how he had never thought about leaving. He had never gone anywhere else either, but the difference was he had no desire. When thinking about the end of the war, his only thoughts were of home, his family, and the Harlows.

The group dispersed. Each man had his task. George was sent on patrol while Christopher and Albert were tasked with digging more trenches and mending the barbed wire that had come undone in places due to shooting. Samuel changed his socks once more and was granted one of his hour-long sleeps of the night. Before sleep consumed him, he wrote his response to Nellie.

Nellie,

Thank you for your letter. I often hope for news of home—even if it's that your work is hard. I'll take any news over another empty day in the trench. Letters are often the only sunbursts of my day, so I was enormously grateful for yours. Although, believe it or not, I think I've made friends here. It's a strange thing to make friends in a war, but I'm thankful for them, nonetheless.

I wish I could have spared you this somehow. I feel as if I've failed as your protective big brother, but I think we both know you would have found a way to nurse and help either way. You were more determined than I had ever seen you when I left, and I'm so proud of you.

You're right. We have all grown up. But I think I see it most in you—our family's little wildflower turned tower of strength. Tell James hello for me. I've written to him, but I'm sure his time is all too occupied to write back soon.

I look forward to the day I can climb out of this hole for good and all of us can return home.

All my love,
Samuel

PS. I'll write to Lillian. I promise.

CHAPTER 12

Lillian paced back and forth across the foyer with her arms folded nervously. She found herself waiting for the post almost daily, although she wasn't quite sure why. She knew good news was rare, and often no news would come at all. But nevertheless, she waited most mornings in the front hall while Mr. Taylor stood by the door at his post—clearly trying not to laugh at the scene. She knew how silly she must look, but she didn't care.

From her place in the hall, she saw the post boy ride up on his bicycle, and Lillian's anxiety grew as Mr. Taylor moved at a glacial pace—smiling all the while. She watched her teasing butler open the door, take the small parcel of letters the boy extended, and shut the door again in one fluid, agonizingly slow motion.

Lillian had written to Samuel the moment he left, but she had heard nothing in response. Under the wartime circumstances, it could be for so many reasons. Perhaps the mail was moving slowly; he'd been captured, injured, or killed; or he simply wasn't responding. She wasn't particularly fond of any of the reasons for his silence. Lillian stood in her robe watching Mr. Taylor fidget with the stack of letters.

"Taylor, good Lord, give me the letters," she finally shouted.

Mr. Taylor chuckled and handed them to her softly. Before walking away, he shot her a smile like he knew something she didn't.

The stack held telegrams for her father, one letter from her nosy grandmother to her mother—undoubtedly asking if Lillian had found a man yet, one letter to her from James, and one, finally, from Samuel. James' letter moved behind Samuel's, and she ripped it open—not even waiting to get upstairs to her bedroom before she started reading.

Lily,

It seems like yesterday and a million years ago we had our first book heist and stole Emma together. Out of all the library raids we accomplished together, that first one will remain one of my favorites.

I don't think you were wrong in seeing them in us. Our friendship was just as special—even back then. You were certainly meddlesome, and I like to think I'm still older and wiser, but I'm sure you would say otherwise. I think our friendship was more important than any ending you might have dreamt. How many of your society friends actually know their gardeners? You know me better than my own family most days. I'm sorry for how I acted that day, but my answer remains unchanged.

I hope you are not suffering at home alone. I know you always hated that. I do not know when my next leave will be or what fate has in store, but I promise I will try my hardest to get back. Check on Nellie every so often—I think you might need each other in the coming days.

Your friend,
Samuel

Lillian finished the letter and continued up the rest of the stairs. She made her way to her bed and sat quietly—contemplating his words. The letter held so many things she needed and so many things she didn't want. He was safe—she knew that now. But his wishes—or at least his answer—had not changed. She sat on the edge of her bed considering all he had said. She wasn't expecting his answer to change, but he wrote it so bluntly. No swish of the pen implied he had struggled with the sentence or didn't want to write it. It just stood there on the page in his scribbled writing and dared her to hurt.

She refused.

She placed the letter back in its envelope and put it on the table beside her bed. She opened the letter from her brother, hoping it would bring better news. It did not.

To my darling sister,

Nothing about this war is what we thought it would be. I see hundreds of men every day, and it's an achievement if even one of them gets to keep all their limbs. Being a doctor here is so different. I've never felt more useless. I keep them alive until they can dictate letters to their loved ones to inform them they won't see them again. I keep them alive long enough to die properly—without shrapnel scattered through their chests.

I didn't think it would be like this—nothing this barbaric. I wanted to follow Daniel like I always have. I wanted to follow him straight into the jaws of death—defending him like he's always defended me. But I can't say I even know where he is now. They sent him to France, last I knew, but I haven't had a letter from him in ages. Samuel is in France as well, but of course they couldn't be together. John is chomping at the bit to join them, although I don't know why. After his birthday, I'm afraid they can send him anywhere. In all honesty, I can't decide which to be more frightened about.

I wish I could spare you all of this, but I've leaned on no one more than you. Don't tell Mother. I don't want her to know the depth of what I have to do. Don't tell Father either. He's finally proud of me for choosing a useful occupation, and while it's never been further from the truth, let's not shatter the glory he most certainly feels for having three sons all serving.

I'm sorry your talk with Samuel didn't go as planned. I'm sure there's more to it than what was said, but you must remember his place is so different from ours. So often we all forget our dearest companions may have grown up with us, lived near us, and maybe even loved us—but they have none of our luxuries or privilege. Of course, I thoroughly hate him for breaking your heart, but try to not to hate him too much yourself. You'll hate yourself if you cast him out.

Please tell me if you hear any word of the others. Of course, they might write me as well, but you can use it as an excuse to keep writing me. I love any and all letters from you. I hope you are well. I hope there are dashing soldiers to entertain you, and I hope four more will join you at home quickly.

Your affectionate brother,
James

She felt for James and the struggle he endured. Ever since he had been refused for service, Lillian didn't look at him with pity but with a sisterly sadness. Her favorite brother was lost—living alone, probably drinking more than he should, most likely spending too much time in the company of young women. Of course, she would never admit to knowing such things, and she knew he would never admit to her accuracy.

Throughout their childhood, she often worried about her brothers. She'd always thought Daniel seemed lost—aimlessly searching for something that would lead him far enough away from his responsibilities. She knew John would be difficult from the moment he drew breath on earth. He found friends who would aid in any destruction he wished. Normally, it involved her father's alcohol and a gathering that started small but ended with broken family heirlooms. She always saw James as steady—the one who kept the four of them grounded, the one who fixed things when they were broken, the one who made a career out of fixing broken people. But when he was refused for active service—each letter showed her more of his downfall and each telephone call sounded less and less like the brother she knew. His letter read well enough, but every word looked shaky, either from exhaustion or intoxication. She hoped Nellie's presence would make him better—or at least make him behave himself.

Her door opened suddenly, shooing her thoughts away. Before the new occupant could see Samuel's handwriting, she stuffed the letter from her table under the pillow beside her. She sat quietly on her bed holding only James' letter. Her mother entered slowly—already dressed for the day ahead and clearly disappointed Lillian was not.

"Lillian, Taylor said you waited for the post again. Is there any word from your brothers?" Her mother had been frantic from the second each of her sons were sent to training or London and out of her reach.

"One from James at the hospital. Nellie's arrived in London now. She's at the hospital with James."

"Never mind that. How is he? When can he get away to come home?"

And you wonder why he writes me instead of you, she thought. She shook her head in response to her mother's questions. Her mother sighed and turned to leave, and Lillian breathed her own sigh. Before her mother exited, she turned back and smiled her tight-lipped grin that implied something horrendous was on the horizon.

"Oh, and get dressed—something pretty. We're expecting company later today for tea."

"What company?" she asked, every cell in her body dreading the response.

"Your father's old school friend Frank Winlen is coming. He's bringing his son, who is home on leave as well."

Lillian was sure her face spoke all the disapproval her stunned lips could not.

"Mother, when are you going to stop throwing men at me?" she said, spitting disdain with every word.

"Perhaps when you catch one." And she was gone.

Lillian sat dumbfounded, and flung herself backward and lay on her bed. Motionless, she held James' letter in one hand and clutched Samuel's under her pillow with the other.

* * *

Lillian had readied herself reluctantly and well into the afternoon just to spite her mother. She pulled on the dress her mother liked best. It was light blue—so light it would have looked white if not for the contrast of the lace pieces that lay over the sleeves and framed the neckline. She pinned her hair up herself. It was the one acquired skill she was genuinely proud of. She piled most of it on top of her head but let a few of her dark curls frame her face and fall down the back of her neck. It was never her goal to appear perfect, and certainly not on a day when her mother planned to present her as such.

How kind that she stays so constant in her efforts even in wartime, she thought as she descended the stairs.

Her mother had trained her to descend the stairs at just the right moment. After all, every young lady deserved an entrance. Lillian had seen the car pull up two stories below under her window that faced the front of the grounds. She saw nothing but the head of an older man followed by an officer's dress cap. She waited the allotted ten minutes after their arrival to exit her room and descend the stairs. The old man nodded and said something to her father about how she had grown, although she had no memory of meeting him before. The uniformed man had his back to her. He was speaking to her mother, obviously trying to impress her, since she was the peddler of her daughter's future. Lillian reached the bottom stair and cleared her throat—irritated by the day's whole arrangement. But when the uniform turned, she caught her breath hard as the soldier made his way to her.

The soldier looked taller than he had from her window and taller still with each step he took toward her. His red hair was light, and the blonde that mingled with it reminded her of orange and golden leaves side by side on autumn trees. His eyes spoke of mischief and sincerity, and Lillian's guard rose higher as she marveled at the handsome stranger. Her mother's voice broke the silence.

"Lillian, dear, this is your father's old friend Frank Winlen," she said, motioning to the old man, who bowed. "And this is Jonah Winlen."

Jonah's eyes met hers, and he bowed low, chuckling the whole way down. As his hand met hers, he looked up and winked at her before speaking. "Miss Harlow, it's a pleasure to meet you."

She wondered if the meeting had equally cornered him. She nodded and smiled in response and took her hand back. The group moved from the foyer to the drawing room for tea. Lillian watched her parents speak with Mr. Winlen and grew increasingly annoyed at their blatant sale of her. Her concentration was interrupted when Jonah sat in the chair closest to her.

"My apologies for this afternoon. Father thinks I should be married, and your mother was all too happy to introduce us." He spoke so plainly Lillian allowed a moment of vulnerability.

"She's all too happy to introduce me to any man of means who isn't too terribly unhandsome."

"Why, Miss Harlow, did you just call me handsome? You must have if I'm here now. My presence must be proof."

Lillian's eyes rolled, but a smirk formed on her lips.

"My dear Mr. Winlen, I have a distinct feeling you have no shortage of women informing you of your charm. I feel no need to increase the number." She watched him shift in his chair. He was clearly surprised by her teasing.

"My father mentioned you had brothers in the service. You must be worried for them," Jonah said.

Lillian was taken aback by the bluntness of his comment but almost appreciated it enough to smile. "I am. All the time. They're all insufferable in their own ways, but I suppose they're good men. What about you? Do you have any sisters or a mother to worry about you?" Her mother heard the question from across the room and coughed loudly. When

Lillian raised her eyes to meet her mother's, she was met with a shake of Mary Harlow's head.

"My mother passed shortly after I was born. Otherwise, I'm sure she would have already planned our engagement with your mother," he said with a smirk. "No siblings either. It's a quiet house for Father, I'm afraid."

Suddenly, Lillian understood the arrangement. A handsome captain ready to inherit some land and a title, no doubt. Lillian shook her head but responded the best she could. "I'm so sorry."

"Don't be. One less person to disappoint, I suppose. Having one parent disapprove is far easier to bear than two." He chuckled, but truth danced behind his eyes.

"And what do you do that is so disappointing, Mr. Winlen?" Lillian disgusted herself with her own flirtation.

Jonah's eyes flashed, but he slid past the question. This was most likely because the answer was not something one said when first introduced, or perhaps ever.

The conversation continued, shifting back to a socially acceptable small talk after her mother coughed again and shot Lillian a glance that scolded her without words. Lillian asked him about where he was last stationed and how he was enjoying his leave. Jonah inquired about the location of her brothers and how she was staying occupied. Each answer was short and polite, but Lillian watched his flirtatious eyes dance. They remained on her for the last moments of the meeting until Jonah's father announced their departure.

"We really must be going," he said as he moved toward the door. "This was wonderful. Thank you for your hospitality."

Lillian's father walked his friend out of the drawing room and through the foyer to the car while her mother followed. Jonah stayed close to Lillian, and the pair followed their merchants.

"Miss Harlow, while this afternoon was clearly orchestrated and nothing would make me happier than ending it in complete disaster—I wonder if I might write to you?"

The question shocked Lillian. It was perhaps the first time in her life she was unsure what to say. Men had always been easy—they wanted her for money or position. She would flirt and move on—eventually refusing them altogether. But Jonah surprised her. His advances were so different from any she had received. How would she handle them?

"Yes, Mr. Winlen, you may write me," she said as he returned his hat to his head. "But whether or not I write you is another matter entirely."

She turned on her heel and let her hands meet behind her as she walked back inside—feeling Jonah's eyes on her with every step.

CHAPTER 13

Lillian watched John closely when he came to home for a visit before receiving his first orders. His birthday was days away—no doubt his duty lay just beyond turning nineteen. Each day that passed inched him closer to his departure. Perhaps for the first time, Lillian worried about him more than anyone else. The days sped by far too quickly for anyone who was not the youngest Harlow.

"It can't get here soon enough, Lillian. I can't wait to get to France." He grinned like a fool.

Lillian shook her head, disappointed but not surprised by her brother's ignorance. Of course, she had no great knowledge of the war herself, but unlike John—she didn't want it.

"John, you have to be careful. It's not a game." She knew at least that much.

"Of course it is, Lillian. Someone wins, someone loses. War is a game with higher stakes—and I always win." He strode away—uniform and all. It simultaneously fit him well while also shrinking him into a small boy. She left him alone with his ignorant dreams of glory.

Her feet led her out the front door and down the familiar path to Samuel's greenhouse. It was theirs, of course, but it always felt more like his—even though he had left it vacant for months. Their correspondence had improved, but she couldn't shake the feeling their relationship had shifted. She could never take back her words, but maybe in time they could learn to ignore what she had declared.

She walked the rows that had now browned with the November winds and snow flurries. The perennials would last through until next year, but she wondered if anyone would be present to tend them when they bloomed again. The longer the war dragged on, the more she wondered how long it would be until it was truly over.

Talk had once swirled about the war only lasting a few months, but now any prediction appeared as foolish as her brother. More than anything, the walk through the emptied greenhouse made her feel farther from her childhood than she ever had. A harsh wind broke Lillian's thoughts and made her wish she had brought a shawl or her coat.

"Miss Lillian?" Mr. Taylor's voice echoed behind her. She turned on her heels to find the familiar butler with his tray. "A letter for you."

"Do you know who from, Taylor?" she asked, but she wasn't quite sure whose name she wanted to hear.

"I believe it's from Captain Winlen, ma'am," Mr. Taylor said with a knowing smile that Lillian returned as she snatched the letter from the tray.

As Mr. Taylor turned to reenter the warm house, Lillian sat on one of the benches that once held Samuel's tools and boots. She felt odd sitting in her friend's safe haven as she held a letter from her handsome new companion. But she shook the thoughts from her head and broke the seal on the letter.

My dear Miss Harlow,

I hope this letter finds you well and not too terribly lonely from my most recent departure. My father mentioned your youngest brother is home before he's given his first orders. I've taken it upon myself to see he enters under the command of my friend, Captain Peter Lorit. He's a good man—he'll watch out for John. Forgive me if I've offended or overstepped. I thought you might want him close to someone you know.

I'm afraid, though, you've been quite unfair. You see, you're quite enchanting, and I've thought of little else since I left you last. Truly, it's the cruelest thing. To make it up to me, please consider doing me the honor of allowing me to escort you to a party on Christmas Eve. I'll be home on leave beginning December 22. Please do not send me back to the trench without the promise of a dance with you.

Give my regards to your mother—I'm sure she'll be thrilled I've written. Perhaps you shouldn't tell her. I have a feeling you dislike being wrong.

Devotedly,
Jonah Winlen

As much as she hated herself for it—she smiled through the whole letter. Jonah's easygoing charm and persistence had worn her down since their first meeting. He was right. She would die before admitting her mother had managed to supply an interesting man she enjoyed being with. Her mother saw only the handsome man in uniform with an inheritance—and a respectable one at that. Lillian's thoughts dragged her back inside to the reality of her life. John stood in the foyer with their mother as Lillian entered a conversation she already desperately wanted out of.

"John, you don't have to go. You took the oath. You went to training. Who says you actually have to go to the front?"

"Um, the king, Mother," Lillian interjected as she thumbed through the remainder of the mail Mr. Taylor had left on the small table in the entryway. Mary Harlow shot her daughter a look of daggers while John chuckled beside her.

"Even if no one had anything to say about it, I'm going," John said proudly.

"But why? You've never been like your brothers. You've never been one to care about duty."

"So wouldn't you be proud of me for caring about it now?" John asked.

"I think everyone knows it's not duty you care about, John. It's glory, and perhaps some blood," Lillian teased, but with weight behind each word.

"And what do you care about, Lillian? Or should I say *who*?" John shot back.

Lillian's head whipped up from the parcel of letters—along with her mother's. In that moment, she knew her annoying little brother had remained the same throughout his training.

"That's none of your business," Lillian said, striding upstairs. But she was followed by her mother and a string of questions.

"What did he mean, Lillian?" she asked all too excitedly.

"Nothing, Mother. It's just a letter."

"You've gotten a few now, haven't you?"

"I suppose. It's correspondence, not a proposal."

Mary Harlow gasped and stopped dead in her tracks. "Lillian, do you mean to say you think there will be a proposal?"

"That's not what I said." Lillian's eyes rolled at her mother's clear motive. "I've just written to him a few times. That's all."

"Well, make sure you don't refuse this one like you have so many others."

Lillian turned slowly, now in front of her door, and spoke quietly but decidedly at her tactless mother. "I refused the others because they wanted my inheritance or the children I would inevitably have to bear for them. I refused the others because they did not respect me, they could not mold me, and they definitely did not love me." She didn't wait for a response. Instead, she entered her room and let the door slam behind her.

She stomped to her small desk by the large window in her room. She wanted so badly to tell Jonah she could not go with him—she *would* not go with him. But how long might it be until she got to dance next? And in truth, she wanted to tell him yes. So she did.

My dear Captain Winlen,

I'm surprised by your invitation but happy to accept. You're right, of course, I won't be telling my mother until absolutely necessary. But she is obviously thrilled you've written, although it wasn't I who told her. As much as I do worry for John—in this present moment I would put him on a ship to France myself. But thank you for securing him a place with someone you trust. It will put my mind at peace—if only for a little while. I'm afraid he's quite keen to fight. He always has been. Captain Lorit will have his hands full.

As much as I hate to admit, I am looking forward to Christmas Eve. But then again, I'm sure I'll see you before then—somehow. You seem to have a knack for popping up unexpectedly. I'm sure this is a trend you won't easily break. Until then, I'll await your reply. Be safe—I don't need another man to worry about.

Yours,
Lillian

As quickly as her pen wrote *yours*, she regretted it. But not enough to change it. Instead, she simply folded it neatly and put it in a small envelope from her drawer. A knock on her door startled her and caused her to stuff the letter in the same drawer as if she was a child hiding something.

"Mother, if it's you—I'm indisposed."

"Lily, it's me, and we both know you're not," John yelled from behind the large door.

Lillian half smiled. Although she was still angry with him, she allowed him to enter. He strode into the room. He had removed his uniform and stood only in his old pair of trousers and a white shirt, unbuttoned at the top against his neck. Lillian hadn't noticed how strong her little brother had become; the lack of uniform made her take note of his growth for the first time in months—even if his maturity had yet to appear.

"I'm sorry, Lil. I didn't mean to unleash Mother on you."

"On the contrary. I think that's exactly what you meant to do—and it worked," she said, standing and crossing to him.

"I didn't want to listen to her telling me to stay. I want to go. I want to do something important."

"You don't have to declare your desire for blood and killing to do something important, you know," she answered.

"I have to talk a big game, Lily. I'm scared." His head hung low as if this was the first time he was saying it out loud. Lillian wondered if it was. "They tell you so much at training. You learn how to shoot, how to stand, how to take orders—but they don't tell you how to kill someone. So I pretend I can do it—because I'm not sure I can."

Lillian saw her brother clearly. He was days away from nineteen and spoke so bluntly to hide the fear he had developed in the months prior. Perhaps at one point the idea of war had truly excited him. But now her little brother stood in front of her admitting his fear.

"Even if you're afraid," she started, "you can go and follow orders bravely. Being afraid does not hinder you from doing the thing you feel is right. Do you feel like it's right? The war?" This question was for herself as much as him.

"I'm not sure, but I know going feels right."

"Then I believe you can, John," she said, smiling.

"I really am sorry, Lil," he said quietly. She knew he was apologizing for more than their mother. His words held a silent "I love you."

"I know." She hugged the littlest Harlow, then watched him turn and leave.

CHAPTER 14

The days spent fighting were short, and the periods of waiting grew longer with each passing day. Samuel's friends had been his great, unexpected joy in war—if there was such a thing. His response to Lillian had brought forth a new thread of letters for which he was grateful. Each one was a bright light for him. The autumn days had overtaken the summer. Now the winter fell bitterly cold on the soldiers each day. December had always meant long days in the greenhouse that warmed him to his core, but now they meant sitting and waiting in the cold for a shot to be fired.

"Perry, mail." The man who delivered the mail was consistent, and it almost made Samuel feel bad for still not having learned his name. Samuel examined the small parcel he received. He wished mail was more reliable. He constantly found himself getting letters out of order or weeks after he sent one. But either way, he accepted each one knowing they would be a momentary escape. The letters held the handwriting of Lillian, Daniel, and Nellie. Samuel tore open Lillian's first—like always.

My dear Sam,

There is nothing much new at all. Mother remains insufferable as ever, though she's mostly concerned about Daniel, James, and John. Now that John has been at the front for almost a month, she's more frantic than ever. I confess I worry about him more than any of you—mostly because I trust the three of you to not intentionally do something stupid. John would go after the Kaiser if he thought it would prove something. He admitted to being frightened before he left. Although I'm sure he would deny it now. But I was happy to know at least for a moment, he saw the depth of what this war means—and the destruction it could cause. I just hope someone, somewhere, is looking after him like you always did here.

Christmas won't feel the same without you here. Nellie is planning on coming home the day after, but James has to stay at the hospital. It'll be nice to have someone here at least. I don't feel right sending your present. I can't guarantee it'll get there in time or even at all. The post has been so unpredictable lately. I'm sure you've already shaken your head at the idea of me getting you a gift. But you're going to love it, and I'll give it to you the first moment you can come home, which I hope is soon.

I've begun reading A Christmas Carol again. Do you remember reading it together last Christmas? I'm not sure either of us could have predicted what the year would hold for both of us. Who would have thought we would have parted for the first time since we've known each other? Or it would have lasted this long? I pray every day it ends quickly. I pray for your safety and the safety of my brothers and so many others.

Try to have a happy Christmas from where you are. I know that might be a lot to ask, or even to hope for, but try.

All my love,
Lily

Samuel read the letter twice through. He shook his head at her gift declaration as she said he would. He had nothing to give her in return, and he had no idea when he would be granted leave. He knew he was being transferred closer to Champagne within days and was confident he would remain there well after Christmas. Leave seemed like a mythical creature—more discussed than ever really seen or experienced.

Samuel tucked the other letters under his leg to keep them from blowing away while he reached for the caramel-colored box. The box had faded in the elements and now looked a dull brown that wasn't nearly as beautiful. He opened it and took out the substantially larger stack of pages and Lillian's letters. He stuck the newest addition under her hair ribbon and closed the lid before turning back to the other messages. He reached for Daniel's first. Samuel had heard so little from him over the past few months he was eager for any news from the eldest Harlow.

Samuel,

I'm so sorry for how little I've written. You and the others have been so faithful with your news, and I, as usual, have shirked my responsibility of doing the same. First let me say I am well. At least as well as I am able to be. I was promoted rather quickly due to the need for more officers, and I fear this is why I have communicated so little.

I am now Lieutenant Harlow. It sounds much more official than it is. I hardly did anything to earn it except perform rather well in training. They needed someone in charge and assumed I would be a suitable fit, although I'm sure I don't know why. Father would undoubtedly laugh at the army's inability to see my lack of ambition or duty. But the odd thing is, I think I feel more sense of duty here than I ever did when I knew I was inheriting my own family's home and lands.

I've been near Flanders until recently and now am back in France. I wish I was able to go home for Christmas, which I'm sure you feel as well. I hope you are well and somehow find some hope and light this Christmas. Who had thought we would spend the holidays of 1914 in a hole in the ground? I pray for you often and hope to see you soon. All my blessings go to you this year, my brother.

Daniel

Samuel stared at the words. He had always been amazed with the way Daniel sounded—well-educated, well-traveled. Clearly nothing had changed on that score. He was thrilled to hear anything at all, but he had never expected the news Daniel was now perhaps ready to face duty. He smiled at the development and turned to the next letter, but the day had fallen into the arms of night, and he could no longer see. Instead, he heard George's voice coming toward him, along with the clunk of his boots.

"Perry, c'mon. We're patrolling tonight."

Samuel tucked Daniel's letter and the rest of his correspondence under Lillian's box to secure them. He grabbed his rifle and his helmet, then stood and followed his friend to the nearest ladder out of the trench. The air blew colder topside, and no-man's-land stared at them like the grim reaper waiting to introduce them to their maker. The ground had long been relieved of the grass that once covered it and instead was now as dark and brown as the trenches they all lived in. Samuel had seen men rise from the trenches and never return. Most times, they disappeared—no word, no gunshots, no anything. It gave new meaning to the phrase "no-man's-land." Samuel held his rifle securely but nervously—only having done a handful of patrols before, he was still unsure of what to expect. George, however, had done hundreds. The pair shuffled past the barbed wire and across the sea of nothingness between them and the German trench.

"Funny," Samuel whispered. "My mum taught me never to eavesdrop, and now I do it to stay alive."

George turned and chuckled at the joke, but he held one finger to his lips with eyes wide, making Samuel stop immediately. The men walked bent down, almost parallel to the ground, all the way to the edge of German territory. Samuel's rifle shifted between his hands due to the sweat that slipped between his fingers. He held it tighter and followed closely behind his friend. He had no idea when they would even get back to their own trench—if they would become one of those who disappeared. Suddenly, he felt terrible for not opening his sister's letter first.

Samuel heard voices not far from where they stood and knew his only job now was to listen, not get shot, and return with what he heard. They lay down quietly and crawled closer to the German trench. Samuel watched George take out a small knife and cut the smallest piece of wire and pocket it. They needed proof they had been there—even if they heard nothing of importance. Of course, neither Samuel nor George spoke German, so instead they watched for any kind of plan, gesture, or familiar name to stand out so they could report it. George motioned to Samuel to move back. He shuffled his legs as fast as he could without making noise and watched as George did the same. George stood quickly and yanked Samuel's collar. Samuel flinched at his friend's cold hand and choked at the strength of the pull.

"What the hell is happening?" Samuel hissed.

"Just shut up and go!" George answered. "One of those damn Germans heard me cutting the wire. I saw him turn."

Samuel knew what that meant. If George had seen one of the Germans, they would have seen him.

George motioned to Samuel and the two of them ran. They didn't sneak or bend low this time. Instead, desperation forced their feet to move faster. Samuel heard yelling behind them and let his legs launch out in front of him—the longest strides he had ever taken. Samuel heard his friend shouting behind him.

"Run, Perry! Don't stop." George pushed him forward, and Samuel dove under the barbed wire and crawled into his trench.

He looked back, and a shot rang out. George's feet stumbled, slamming him face-first onto the barbed wire in front of the British trench. Samuel stood stunned. He began to crawl back out but felt two strong hands on his back that kept him down. He turned to find Albert pulling him down the ladder into the trench.

"George is still out there! He might be alive!"

"Shut up, will you? We'll get him when we can, but if you crawl up there now, then you're both dead for sure!"

The shooting continued for another fifteen minutes, but Samuel felt each minute drag on for an hour at least. When the blasts finally stalled, the men waited, in case the enemy was trying to draw them out. A lookout on the other side of the trench motioned the all clear, and Samuel and Albert climbed out to retrieve their comrade.

Albert crawled under the wire and untangled George carefully. His limbs flopped like they were never even connected to the rest of him. Samuel could barely see through the dark, but as Albert pushed George closer to him, he saw the blood caking his face and arms. Blood spots stained his trousers, betraying more punctures under his uniform. George was certainly just unconscious—no doubt from the pain. As Samuel finally pulled his friend all the way down into the trench, he understood George lay lifeless in his arms. Samuel took the piece of wire from his friend's pocket and handed it to Albert once he too was back in the trench.

"We were there. They saw him getting this," he said.

Albert nodded. "He knew the risk of getting proof."

Samuel shook his head and waited with George until the medical unit retrieved him. Even though his heart had stopped, the blood seemed to flow in a constant stream from the wounds on his body. Samuel had seen the nameless men beside him die, but not yet one he had called a friend. As blood poured freely from one of George's eyes and melded with a wound in the front of his neck, Samuel knew he had witnessed a death that killed him too.

* * *

Samuel trudged back to his tiny hovel and slammed his helmet down hard enough for it to stick in the soft ground. He slammed himself down and laid his head in his hands. Every discussion of life after the war came instantly to his memory, and regret filled every crevice of his mind. He reached for Nellie's letter and opened it, hoping for some relief from the night he had endured.

Sammy,

I hope you are well. I know you probably won't receive another letter from me before Christmas, so Merry Christmas. I wish you were here and we were fighting over who would get the biggest helping of Mum's pudding.

The hospital is much the same. Men still come in, and only a fraction of them walk out again. Even if they do walk out, they're rarely whole. I think I've become immune to the sadness this work brings. It's all factual. I come in each morning, and sometimes I haven't even left in the night. I see men bleeding and dying and I do my best. But sometimes it's not enough.

I'm not sure if anyone told you yet or if you heard word somehow, but John has been injured. He was shot and had shrapnel spread throughout his leg. They had to amputate just below his knee. He was barely there, and now I fear he'll hardly be here anymore either. He's coming home to recuperate and learn to manage. No doubt he'll struggle more than we know.

Please make sure we don't hear any similar news about you. Don't try to be a hero. I love you.

Your affectionate sister,
Nellie

Samuel crumpled the letter in his hand and threw it into the standing water at his feet. His head returned to his hands. He had just watched one of his friends die before his eyes, only to learn his adopted brother had lost a leg in the same day. He wondered how many more men would be injured or lost altogether. He feared the number.

His final letter laid beside him. Samuel stared at it—completely unsure of its contents and worried what the paper might contain. He wasn't sure he could endure more news of loss before morning. He lit a cigarette, still looking at the letter, and finally decided to rip it open as he took two big puffs.

Private Samuel Arthur Perry is granted four days of leave beginning December 28, 1914, at 0800 hours.

Samuel finished his cigarette, smiling for the first time all night.

CHAPTER 15

Lillian had spent the last several nights tossing and turning rather than sleeping. She had felt guilty even longer. She told Samuel nothing was new—which of course wasn't true. Everything was new. Everything was different. Their hill, the greenhouse that always felt more like Samuel's than her own, Jonah and her growing feelings for him, John's change since his injury—nothing was the same.

Jonah had not been granted leave to visit until the night of the party. That was just as well, because Lillian wasn't sure if she was nervous, excited, or anxious about seeing him again. They had written more than she thought they would. He was kind and charming as ever, and Lillian hated herself for how impatiently she waited for each letter to arrive. She hated herself more for the joy she felt when Christmas Eve finally arrived.

She slipped on her yellow robe and moved to the vanity. Only a few pictures adorned it—one of her brothers and her, one of her parents, and her siblings and her with the Perry children. Her mother had insisted on at least one photograph of the six of them in their lifetime. It had been taken the summer before the war, but she stared at it, noticing how young they all looked. The world had certainly changed each one of them. She sighed as she thought about how much had happened. Daniel was rising through the ranks. James was serving in the only way he could. She had confessed her feelings to Samuel, who had left as well. John had returned broken in more ways than one, and Nellie consistently tried to put him and countless others back together again.

Lillian let her thoughts retreat from her mind and she dressed in a crisp white dress shirt and pulled on one of her warmest skirts of a deep navy and a light blue knit sweater that accentuated her tiny waist. She descended the stairs without bothering with her hair. She let it fall loose over her shoulders in the mess of curls she rarely wanted to tame. She had no real need to look perfect for breakfast. Shortly after, her mother would usher her up the stairs and spend the following hours creating the perfection she demanded. She stopped only a few stairs from the bottom when she heard a familiar voice coming from the library.

"Thank you, sir."

Jonah's voice—muffled from behind the door. Lillian positioned herself only steps away. She nervously fiddled with her ensemble, realizing this would be the most casual Jonah had ever seen her when he exited the door. Part of her wanted to hide. The other was ready to confront whatever was taking place inside the library.

The door opened and Lillian stood straighter—facing Jonah and her father. For a man who was less than affectionate, she was surprised to find her father's hand on Jonah's shoulder. Her father slipped by her without a glance and walked straight to the dining room without a word. She shifted her eyes to Jonah. He stood in front of her, leaning on the door frame with a smug smile plastered across his face. She stepped toward him slowly, letting her arms swing around and meet behind her back.

"You're not supposed to be here until tonight. Did you change your mind already, Captain Winlen?" she flirted.

Jonah pulled his hat from under his arm as he chuckled. "On the contrary, Miss Harlow. I assure you my mind is quite made up."

He stepped toward her until only air separated them. She looked up at him, watching his mischievous face look down at her and wink. Then without a pause, he turned on his heels and exited the house, leaving Lillian alone—breathless in the foyer.

* * *

Lillian spent the rest of the day with her mother underfoot. She had used the better part of the afternoon to remind Lillian of every single thing she had ever taught her about being a proper lady.

"Mother, I've already had my debutante ball—this is just another party."

"Yes, but how many more will you attend unmarried before you're tossed aside?"

"Tossed aside how?"

"For being an old maid," her mother responded, choking back a false sob.

"Oh, gracious, Mother. I'm twenty-one! Plenty of older girls get married."

"And are their wedding photographs as beautiful? No. They're older than they should be—and they lose vital years when they could be having children."

Well, at least her priorities are in order, Lillian thought with a roll of her eyes. She sighed and attempted to usher her mother out of the room so she could dress. But mostly so she could be rid of her for a few moments.

"But, Lillian, I can help you. I can—"

"Mother," Lillian began. "Leave this instant or I won't wear a corset like the women in London."

Mary Harlow flew from the room.

Lillian sighed with relief as one of the maids entered to help her dress. Even with the corset fully knotted and secured, in that moment, Lillian breathed easier than she had the entire day.

She slipped into a dress of emerald velvet. It fell over her ivory skin gently and softly. The gown was extravagant for wartime, but she had always loved Christmas and wanted to make the best effort she could. The sleeves puffed just the right amount and the skirt hung loose rather than being bustled, which allowed her to turn and twirl like she had as a girl. She pinned her hair up herself and, like always, let her signature curls fall in all their bouncing glory. She took her gloves from the maid and descended the stairs to meet Jonah for the second time that day.

Instead of teasing, Jonah simply smiled. His genuine grin made her giggle and stand a bit straighter as she took the last step to meet the ground. He draped her coat around her shoulders and led her out into the night.

* * *

Lillian stepped out of the car, holding Jonah's hand as he led her into a mansion that rivaled her own. She looked up at the windows, which seemed to multiply the higher they rose. A large, crystal chandelier shone through the December night.

After being relieved of her coat at the door, she slipped her gloved hand inside Jonah's again. The pair entered the ornate room where beautiful people, candles, and bright red poinsettias engulfed them. Lillian's gaze lifted to meet the crystals she had seen from outside. Garland and greenery dripped from fireplaces, and Lillian could see at least three Christmas trees from only feet inside the first room. For the first time in her life, she understood how Samuel and Nellie must have felt entering her own home for the first time.

"Do you like it?" Jonah whispered, putting his mouth much closer to her ear than it needed to be.

"It's stunning," she answered, looking down at her feet—refusing to turn and meet his gaze.

"I'm glad," he started. "I wonder—"

"Winlen! You rat!" Another uniformed man yelled from behind them. "How dare you walk in here with the best-looking girl!"

Lillian clenched her jaw as she turned to meet a lanky man with a small mustache and mind to match. *Why must they always think that's the compliment we want to hear?*

"Lillian, meet Captain Peter Lorit."

She stiffened. "The same Captain Lorit who led my brother John?"

"The very same, ma'am," Lorit answered—kissing her hand, which she had not offered.

"I wonder if you spent more time leading than attempting to flatter women, my brother might have both his legs," she said, pulling her arm back. Jonah laughed beside her, but she did not turn to face him or quiet him. Instead, she put her hand on top of her other and clasped his arm firmly.

"I can't win every battle, ma'am—and I can't save every man," Lorit spat back. His words slurred. He had clearly already had too much champagne.

"Well, let's hope His Majesty the King doesn't share your view, or the Kaiser will have us beat by the new year. Excuse us." She pulled Jonah farther into the room of dancing couples. Her anger caused her to shake, and she wondered if Jonah could feel it.

"I should thank you. Peter's always insufferable at these things. He probably won't speak to another soul all evening." Jonah's teasing confirmed she had said just enough.

"He's pompous and arrogant."

"Yes, but a good captain."

"Somehow I doubt that," she answered, thinking of John at home. He hadn't moved in days, and rarely spoke more words than necessary.

Jonah nudged her gently. "Cheer up, Lily. This is supposed to be a party."

She looked up at him—confused at how it felt so natural for someone beside Samuel to call her *Lily.* She smiled and led him to the dance floor. The pair circled and twirled. She held Jonah's right hand in her left, thinking his other hand held more tightly to her waist than was acceptable. But she didn't mind.

The music stopped and Jonah took her hand, threaded it through the crook of his arm, and led her back through the foyer. She marveled at the chandelier once again and caught sight of a familiar face descending the stairs.

"Merry Christmas, Father," Jonah said, shaking his father's hand with his free one.

"Merry Christmas, my boy. Miss Harlow, you look stunning," he began. "I do hope you'll join us here again for the new year. You and your family will be most welcome, even though Jonah's leave will have ended by then."

"Back here? But—"

"We should be going, Father," Jonah interrupted. "I'm going to show Miss Harlow the library." And he led her away.

"You failed to mention this was your party *and* your house," she said as they walked.

"Did I?" he answered with a smirk as his hand slipped behind her and pointed her through a large door. Books towered above their heads, and a small balcony held at least fifty more stacks. The small ladder with worn wheels beside the lower shelves proved the room was well-loved. She stepped farther in alone. Lights littered the shelves—almost as many of them as there were books. Lillian wondered how a place as grand as this one could be a home—it felt more like a dream.

Lillian spun and found Jonah behind her on a bended knee.

"Jonah . . ." Her breath caught when her eyes met the ring in his hand. The gold band was topped with a light pink sapphire and two small diamonds on each side that bled into the intricate, woven design of rest of the ring.

"Lillian," he said, standing. "I'm sorry, I was going to do this conventionally—the right way. But you're not conventional. I'm not conventional. The two of us definitely are not."

"No." She laughed. "I don't believe we are."

"This is what our parents wanted. I'm not blind to that. But I'm not doing this because it's what they want. I've wanted to ask you since the moment you teased me back when we first met. You're bold. You can certainly handle yourself—and me. I'm not asking because I want your money—I have plenty of my own coming to me someday. And I don't need your family name—I'm hoping you'll accept mine." He stood only inches from her now. In all the proposals she had heard and refused, his speech was by far the best—and the most truthful. She searched for a response and found none suitable.

"It's beautiful, Jonah," she said, looking at the ring, trying to decide what her next words would be.

Jonah chuckled. "I would lie and say it's a family ring, but it's not. Father wanted me to give you my great-grandmother's ring, but it wasn't right. I had this one made weeks ago. Your reputation proceeds you. I knew you'd seen a fair number of rings, so I thought I would make one that was hard to turn down."

She laughed. He thought of everything—as always. But mostly, he had thought of her, and not what she could give him.

"Jonah, I—"

"You don't have to answer now. You can take whatever time you need. I hope to have a few days leave in the coming months, and you can give me your answer then."

She laughed again. In the short time she had known him, he had never been nervous—always confident and sure. But the longer she left him without an answer, the more bumbling his speech became. She knew she had to put him out of his misery. So she did.

"Jonah," she said, moving closer. "Yes."

And she smiled.

"Oh, thank God." Jonah let out a sigh and bent down—pushing his lips onto hers as if they needed to be there. When he finally backed away, Lillian looked up at him slowly.

"So do I get to wear that now?" she teased.

Jonah smirked and slid the blinding ring on her left hand.

"When will you tell your family?" he asked.

"Oh, not for a few days, I think. I'll let my mother believe I refused another perfectly adequate proposal."

"Adequate? Why, Miss Harlow—you've offended me."

She giggled and stretched up to peck his cheek. "It was lovely."

Jonah's smile covered more of his face than she had ever seen as he led her back out to the party. Congratulations flew freely and frequently. The men clapped Jonah on the back for securing the most elusive girl in the county while the women gathered around Lillian's hand to see the stunning pink stone. Lillian smiled at her fiancé across the sea of people.

Questions swirled around her. Each woman asked what her dress would be like, what her parents would think, if they had settled on a date already, and more. Only one question stopped Lillian's blind joy.

"Where will you get your wedding flowers?

"Oh, our garden, I suppose," she answered, not entirely thinking.

"Of course," the unknown woman replied. "That Perry boy had such a gift."

Lillian nodded, but her smile faltered for a moment. She wished for the first time Samuel would not return home anytime soon.

CHAPTER 16

Samuel had been in Champagne for over a week now, and Christmas was on the horizon. With his leave so close, Christmas in the trenches seemed almost tolerable. Christopher had been sent to Belgium. But Albert remained in France with him, for which he was grateful.

Samuel's leave notice had introduced a glimmer of hope into the deep sadness and monotony that hung over the days since George's death. Albert had come to him multiple times with cards in hand, but they both must have felt the loss of their other players, because the deck was never dealt. Instead, the pair only talked and tried to laugh. Now talk never shifted to what would happen after the war, rather only what came before. Nostalgia was simpler and safer than wishes or dreams for the future.

He had started so many letters home to tell everyone about his four days leave. But as the cold days continued, and his excitement grew—he wished for nothing but to surprise everyone at home. So he wrote no one and told no one of his plans. He hoped for a happy surprise. His anticipation grew as each day crept closer and closer to December 28.

Samuel had requested and been granted fewer patrols for the time being. After George's death, the idea of traveling under the wire again frightened him even more than the looming threat of bullets or grenades. Thankfully, his superiors didn't think he was in the right condition to patrol. They would rather he remain a body in the trench rather than a corpse outside of it. Instead, Samuel worried and watched almost every time Albert went out. As much as he and the other men hated the trench—at times it felt like the closest of companions and greatest of protectors.

Night fell more quickly since winter had made its official entrance into France. The nights felt long—waiting for bullets, patrols, or raids. But the days were even longer when they were forced to fill the time themselves. Samuel chose to sleep the little bit he could through the early morning. After the night of watching for Albert to return, Samuel allowed his eyes to finally close for the first time in over twenty-four hours. His sleep was deep enough to be dreamless, which was a rare and true gift. But the gift didn't last, as Albert shook Samuel awake.

"Perry. Wake up."

"What the hell, Blake? I just got here. Let a man sleep." And he lowered his helmet over his eyes again. Only a moment passed before the helmet was lifted from his face completely. He could feel the sun's rays sit on his eyelids and kept them closed. "You better put my bloody helmet down or you're going to lose that hand."

"What would Anna Perry say to such a comment?"

Samuel's eyes snapped open at the familiar voice speaking his mother's name. Daniel Harlow stood before him in full uniform with a smile wider than the distance between Champagne and home.

"Daniel!" Samuel struggled to his feet and saluted his friend the lieutenant. Daniel smiled and grabbed Samuel for their first embrace in months. Samuel patted the eldest Harlow on the back and released him from the hug.

"I've been looking for you all morning," Daniel said with a smile. "My men and I arrived here today, and I heard from your superiors you were here as well. You boys dug in nicely—I've looked for over an hour."

Samuel smiled at the familiarity of his friend. He had to spend Christmas in the trenches, but at least he'd spend it with one piece of home. Samuel and Daniel talked through most of the day as it bled into evening.

"I'll be Captain Harlow in a month or two. It's all quite funny when you think about it. But like I wrote to you, I think I feel proud of something I've done for the first time. Truly, I think I could find purpose doing this."

Samuel watched his friend become passionate about an occupation for the first time in his life, and felt a sense of brotherly pride and excitement for what the future held for both of them.

"I'm happy for you, Daniel. I hope everything works out for you—I really do."

"What about you, Sam? What do you want? What does life look like for you after the war?"

Samuel dreaded the question, both for the fate it tempted and the answer he didn't have.

"I suppose I'll go home—back to your home—and do what I've always done. I've always been the gardener boy, and I think it might be the best thing for me." He spoke quietly but not sadly. It was simply a fact. He was the gardener boy, and he never once felt his role was a negative one. He had inherited it from his father. It wasn't an estate or lands like Daniel would have, but it was his. The only time he wished it wasn't, was the day he left—the day Lillian asked him for the impossible.

"It won't be the same when we get back. The expectations won't be the same, Sam."

"What do you mean? Of course the expectations will be the same."

Daniel shook his head. "But they won't. Men of all backgrounds enlisted. We're all here in the trenches together. Class will still be there—I'm not sure if it will ever truly disappear completely. But it won't be nearly as important as we thought it was before the war. Your role could change if you want it to—I know it could."

Samuel considered every word of Daniel's speech and pondered its accuracy.

"That sounds nice for you, Daniel. But I'm not sure if that's true for me. Your family tends to forget I don't have half of the privileges you do. I've never had the freedom you have."

"You're right. We all forgot you and Nellie didn't have the freedoms we did. But I think soon you could—at least maybe more than before. I hope you do."

Daniel spoke with a sincerity Samuel found hope in. If the new world Daniel envisioned became reality, he knew so much would change—so much *could* change. Night had finally choked the light out of the day, but Samuel and Daniel still sat together—reminiscing, dreaming, and hoping. Samuel was grateful for his friend's wish—the wish for a better world, a more accepting one.

A world Samuel could join, and he wished the same. The patrols went out and a raid was set to follow. Daniel would lead his men, and Samuel readied himself to climb out of the trenches again. Every watch struck midnight, and before Daniel left, Samuel yelled to his friend from the trench.

"Merry Christmas, Daniel."
"Merry Christmas, Sam."

* * *

The raid never happened. Samuel climbed out of the trench with the other men on Christmas morning, ready to be met with gifts of bullets and grenades from the Germans. But none came. Instead, throughout the stillness of the early hours, he heard "Silent Night" from across no-man's-land.

Samuel had heard the reports like every other man. A truce had been suggested for Christmas Day, but not one man in the trench ever thought it would become a reality. Samuel was no different from the others. He wished for it to be true, but nothing led him to believe it was. But the Germans singing Christmas carols across barbed wire and bodies made the faint hope a reality.

He stood with the British army, waiting for a trick. A cease-fire seemed too good to be true, and a moment of blind trust could mean every one of their deaths and a German victory on the Western Front. Samuel, along with the other troops, feared a German victory perhaps even more than losing his own life. They waited deep into the morning. The sun had risen to cast the smallest bit of warmth Samuel and the others had craved for so many days and weeks. Suddenly, when the Germans finally stopped their song, one soldier started again. But now, in response, the Allies sang "Silent Night" in English.

From the German trench, "Silent Night" was sung again, and Samuel paused—completely silent as the song suggested. While it was no longer night—it did feel holy. Samuel heard a softness in the voice of each singing man and a hope in each silent rifle.

As the sun shone high, the next words became true as well. Everything felt calm for the first time in months, and the men were grateful for it. Samuel walked forward, his gun hanging in his arms until it dropped on the ground altogether. From across the chasm, his enemies did the same. The calmness consumed them, and each man welcomed it willingly—undoubtedly hoping it would last longer than Christmas Day.

Samuel watched as Daniel moved down the row of British soldiers. The two of them walked together toward the Germans, but for once felt no fear of death or retaliation. The opposing army suddenly flowed across no-man's-land. Samuel felt tension rise beside him, but not one man reached for their gun or moved at all. Instead, they only listened.

"Merry Christmas!" the soldiers facing them yelled.

"Merry Christmas!" Samuel heard his own voice ring out.

The Germans moved closer, but this time each British soldier took steps toward them as well. The lines of men who crawled from the trenches approached each other unarmed and confused but strangely joyous. Every man stalled when the Allies met the Central Powers in the middle of the dangerous abandoned ground.

Samuel stood face-to-face with a German and feared nothing. Instead, he smiled. The man opposite him did the same. Samuel extended his hand slowly and waited, unmoving. The man took it, and they stood as comrades for the first, and perhaps the only time. From either side, men followed and joined hands with their opponents. Laughter burst from Samuel's chest, and he looked at the sky that covered the scene, wondering if anyone would believe the sight.

The lines of men suddenly blurred, and Samuel saw and heard the trading of cigarettes and stories around him. He felt a clap on his back and knew at once it was Daniel. He turned to face him and smiled.

"Who had thought I would shake hands with a German today?" Samuel asked.

Daniel laughed and looked around at the scene Samuel had been admiring.

"I told you," Daniel started, "the world won't be the same when this is over."

And in that moment, Samuel believed him.

CHAPTER 17

The Christmas truce didn't last. Even though it extended into December 26, by the following day, bullets flew again as if nothing had happened. Samuel had never been more grateful for his leave than the day the war resumed. December 27 was the longest day of Samuel's life. His morning was spent packing the little he had with him. The final thing to enter the bag was Lillian's wooden box.

The afternoon was filled with cigarettes and anticipation. Samuel said little and tried to think of a time he had been more ready to return to his little piece of the world. But none existed. Albert continuously brought him back to reality—teasing all day long to remind him he had to come back to the trenches eventually.

"You gonna see that girl you keep writing?" Albert asked with a knowing smile.

Samuel rolled his eyes but looked down with a grin. He would see Lillian in a few short hours. "I might."

"C'mon, Perry. You said you didn't have a girl when you came here, but those letters come and go faster than most."

Albert baited him—fishing for any information Samuel was willing to give. But the nosiness made Samuel prickle ever so slightly. By not disclosing any information about her, he felt he was protecting her, but also, he shielded his own feelings. He didn't need anyone else convincing him he could pursue something with her when he knew nothing at all was to be done. But either way, he started talking.

"Her name is Lillian, if you must know. I worked for her family back home. We've been friends since we were young. She's genuinely one of the most stubborn girls you'll ever meet, and no doubt she'll be furious I didn't tell her I was coming home." Samuel smiled at the last part, knowing it to be true, and laughed when he imagined the response.

Albert shot a smirk at him from where he leaned against the side of their trench, but he said nothing. He only shook his head.

Samuel could have asked him what he was thinking, but he didn't much feel like negating any comment that might come. So instead, he simply turned back to packing and dreamt of the next morning.

* * *

Samuel prepared to leave France at exactly 0800 hours. He didn't want to waste a moment getting back to English soil. The day began slowly with a boat ride across the English Channel that felt eternal and even more soul-crushing than the long days in the trenches. Although, it did give him a moment to sleep soundly for the first time without the fear of waking up to another raid or bullets catching him. The boat docked in London, and Samuel woke with a start as travelers bustled around him. He rose, standing tall in his uniform, put on his cap, and slung his bag over his shoulder.

Samuel had only been to London a handful of times in his life, but stepping off the boat into England made him feel like he was really truly home. It was bitterly cold, but Samuel didn't mind. Docking in London gave him the opportunity to see Nellie and James before returning home to his mother and the Harlow estate. It was the only stop he would dream of making before setting foot on his childhood soil. He pulled Nellie's letters from his pack to remember the exact London hospital that kept her so busy. So many hospitals had popped up in the months since the war started—the need for more doctors and beds kept growing. He couldn't be certain which one was correct on his own. The steps to the hospital were grand and clearly indicated it was the original hospital building, but he knew it didn't hold the ailments it used to.

Samuel timidly walked into the building and was stopped by the stench of metal that only surgical instruments and blood could hold. Nurses dodged him and darted from one room on his left full of men on cots barely held together to the room on his right that held men lying side by side waiting for attention. Samuel had witnessed men die in front of him and sustain numerous injuries, but they were always carried away as swiftly as possible. He was never forced to watch the decay or hear the wailing of men in pain. His heart raced and his breathing quickened and shallowed as his mind turned to George—the death that haunted him the most. In his mind, he saw his friend fall slowly onto the mountain of barbed wire that was supposed to protect them. A familiar voice broke his moment of terrified remembrance.

"Samuel!" James' voice rang from across the sea of bodies. He stepped over them with practiced precision. Samuel wondered if James looked more weathered from the war than he did. Someone's blood stained the coverings he wore, and darkness sat comfortably under his eyes like it had made a home in his skin.

"James. How are you?" A stupid question, but one everyone asked.

"Well, I've only had three deaths so far today, so we're hopeful."

At only ten thirty in the morning, Samuel feared what the other hours of the day might hold.

"Would you happen to know where my little sister is?"

James smiled like he held a secret between his lips he dared not speak. Samuel shifted his gaze as James nodded to the room behind Samuel's back. He turned slowly to see Nellie, now almost twenty, changing a man's bandages. She wiped her brow and turned the man on his side to tend the wound on the soldier's back. Samuel stood amazed at the woman he watched. He stayed stationary and gazed at the simple, growth-filled scene. Nellie possessed the same careful care their mother had shown when nursing their dying father. He suddenly felt abundant pride to belong to both the Perry women. When Nellie had finally dressed the wound, she stood slowly and met his eyes.

"Sammy!" Her professionalism left suddenly as she leapt over men to race to him. She jumped into his embrace like no time had passed and slapped his arm the moment he set her down. "Why didn't you tell us you were coming?"

"I didn't tell anyone. I had to stop here before going home. I have four days before I have to be back in France."

Nellie's eyes shifted to James. "You haven't been home yet? Have you written Mum? Or Lillian? Or anyone?"

"No? I thought it would be a nice surprise." Samuel was baffled by Nellie's mysterious tone. Before he had time to ask what she meant, an ambulance skidded to a stop in front of the hospital steps. Chaos ensued. He watched his sister rush down the steps like clockwork and heard James' voice call after her.

"Nurse Perry, I'll tend to the amputations first. For anyone who passes before treatment, find their home addresses and write their families."

Samuel shuddered at the flippancy of each statement—like death meant nothing except one more letter to write. In a way, the hospital was as savage as the trench.

"Nellie, I'll be at home," he called after his sister, but he was certain she didn't hear him. He grabbed his pack and started for the train station. He looked back one last time at his sister with disbelief.

She's incredible, he thought.

And he continued on.

* * *

Samuel reached Staffordshire by noon. While his travels took almost no time at all, each minute felt longer than the last until he finally began the familiar journey down the lane to the Harlow estate. Each step made him want to run to the house, but he forced restraint, and his mind raced in front of him instead. He wasn't sure what state John would be in or how Lillian would react to his presence. They hadn't seen each other since that day at the train, and all the letters in the world couldn't prepare him to face her again.

With the estate in sight, he allowed his steps to hasten until he reached the door knocker that felt like a friend in itself. He slammed it down three times and stood straight at attention on the front steps. As he waited, he noticed a car that did not belong to the Harlow family—at least it didn't when he left. Mr. Taylor opened the door like always, and his feet nearly fell out from under him when he saw Samuel.

"Samuel! My dear boy, no one told us you were coming. We saw you coming up the walk." The smile that emerged on Mr. Taylor's face pleased Samuel to no end.

"I didn't tell anyone myself. Not even my mother. I met James and Nellie at the hospital, then came here directly." He smiled and strode inside as Mr. Taylor moved aside to reveal the familiar foyer. "Did the family get a new motor?" He asked, referring to the vehicle he had passed. Mr. Taylor shook his head, and, before he answered completely, Frederick Harlow greeted Samuel.

"Samuel! Thank goodness you're alright." Mr. Harlow shook his hand and motioned to the library. Samuel walked slowly. He felt ushered away somehow and was unsure why he felt so unwelcome for the first time in his life. Mary Harlow stood in the room, waiting.

"We're happy to see you, Samuel. We hoped to catch you before you interrupted."

"Interrupted?" Samuel asked. The Harlow parents exchanged a knowing look but said nothing.

"Lillian is entertaining."

Samuel nodded. He had often come into contact with Lillian's society friends—women who were debutantes the same year. She was usually thankful for the interruption, but he wasn't eager to meet them again. He preferred to see her again with the other ladies gone. He stood strong and tall while the Harlow parents took in the sight of him. They smiled, but only halfway and halfheartedly. The minutes passed slowly until a total five had passed. Mrs. Harlow moved toward him.

"Samuel, your mother will be expecting you. We'll tell Lillian and John you're home. They'll make their way to you soon, I'm sure." She motioned toward the door on the opposite side of the library. He felt cornered but had never opposed the woman before and was not eager to begin. Just as he was about to take his final steps out of the library and the house, the library door opened.

"Mother, Jonah and I—" and Lillian's voice halted as Samuel turned to face her. "Sam? Is it really you?" Her voice grew weak, like tears were forming in the back of her throat.

He simply nodded—unable to speak himself. He readied himself to be attacked with an embrace like his meeting with Nellie, but Lillian stayed planted. The room tensed, but Samuel could not determine why.

"My dear, let's leave them for a moment." Mr. Harlow spoke and ushered his wife out. She protested and shot Lillian a glance.

War has truly changed expectations, Samuel thought as Frederick Harlow left his unmarried daughter in a room alone with him. The door shut and Samuel moved forward.

"Lily, I'm here. It's me."

"It's you. How are you here?"

"I received four days leave. I wanted to surprise everyone."

"Well, you certainly did." She laughed lightly and moved to meet him, grasping his hand and squeezing slightly.

Samuel felt his breathing relax at her touch, and he allowed himself to embrace her for the first time in months.

"Samuel, I have to tell you something."

Samuel stepped back slowly, putting the pieces of the afternoon together in his mind.

"Lily, who does the motor out front belong to?" His hand slid into hers, and he felt a large stone on her ring finger.

Lillian took a sharp breath in as the door opened behind her. A uniformed man—of higher rank than himself—appeared. Samuel looked from him to Lillian, then saluted and offered a nod. Lillian's eyes closed slowly and did not open again until the unknown soldier finally spoke.

"I'm Captain Winlen. And you are?"

"Private Perry," Samuel answered, not taking his eyes from Lillian.

"Lillian, your mother says the luncheon is ready," he said, not moving from his spot at the door.

"Thank you, Jonah . . . um . . . Captain Winlen. Please tell her I'll be right there." Her eyes finally opened as she corrected how she addressed her visitor.

Captain Winlen exited and left Samuel alone with Lillian. He moved away and turned his back to her.

"So you're engaged?"

"Did you really expect me to be heartbroken and alone until the war ended?"

Her irritation nearly flipped him around on its own. He took a brisk step toward her.

"And you didn't think to tell me?"

"You would have found out eventually. It happened only days ago—it wasn't as if I was hiding it." Her voice rose with each sentence and she moved closer, inches from his face.

"But you did. You said there was nothing new. What did you do? Take up with the first man you saw after I left?"

"Do you really think so highly of yourself? Did you expect me to wait? Or die an old maid? I'm not that helpless, Sam," she spat. "You were not here. He was. Mother introduced us. He became a good friend. We wrote to each other. He's kind and respects me and has the credentials my family needs to approve. So I said yes."

"So he has money? And a title, I'm assuming?" he asked.

She simply nodded.

"I must marry sometime. I'd rather it be a friend. You said it could not be you. He's my friend. He's charming and kind and he's honest. He's never hidden anything from me, and I've never hidden anything from him." She spoke plainly and without sympathy.

"So you told him? You told him about that day?" he asked.

Silence.

"He knows about you. He knows we were close. He knows I care about you. That's all he needs to know. Nothing else happened—you said it couldn't," she whispered.

"Well, your fiancé is waiting. And luncheon and your parents' wishes and expectations. And your future," he said, turning to stride from the room.

"Not one part of that is fair, Sam," she said.

He paused.

"You're right, Lillian. Not one bit of this is fair," he said quietly. Then he exited.

CHAPTER 18

Samuel all but ran through the front door. He never once looked back to see if Lillian was following him, but in his heart, he knew she wasn't. Of all the things he thought awaited him at home—an engaged Lillian was not one of them. The walk back down the lane felt slower than any he had taken before. His pack felt heavier with every step toward home, and his mind swarmed with guilt over his words, regret over the ones he left unsaid, and a million memories and questions. With his home in sight, his steps quickened until he was in front of his door. He stopped, unsure if he should knock. Strangely, the last exchange made him feel as if he no longer belonged in Staffordshire.

He knocked.

His mother opened the door and froze. She held a mixing bowl, undoubtedly full of delicious batter that would turn into a treat for a neighbor. Samuel chuckled as the bowl fell to the ground and his mother flung her arms around his neck. This was the welcome he needed.

"You stupid boy! Why didn't you tell me you were coming?" his mother asked, releasing him.

"I didn't tell anyone. I thought it would be a nice surprise. I saw Nellie and James at the hospital, and I just came from the Harlow estate," he said, stumbling over the last bit.

"Oh? So you met—?"

"The captain? Yes," Samuel answered, shuffling past his mother. He picked up the bowl from the ground and scooped up as much of the mixture as he could to dispose of it. His mother watched him, waiting for more of a response, but he could think of no words, even if he wanted to talk.

He looked around the space and wondered how he had ever lived there. It felt like a lifetime ago. His mother followed him, closing the door. She made her way to the kitchen table where she mixed her ingredients again.

"It happened on Christmas Eve," she said quietly—answering the question he hadn't asked but had wanted to.

"How long have they—"

"Only a little while, but I suppose no one wants to waste time. No one knows how long this war will last. You can't blame them for wanting to speed things along."

"I didn't even know about him, Mum. She didn't tell me," he said, finally sitting and laying his hat on the table.

"Was she supposed to, Sam?" his mother asked with a knowing look.

Samuel had no answer. He simply shook his head and let it hang—partially in exhaustion and partially in defeat.

"I have to go back."

"Don't you dare, Samuel Arthur Perry!" His mother's voice bellowing his middle name made Samuel's head snap up. "They're happy. They're getting married. Don't go spoiling things."

Samuel's mother was more observant than he had given her credit for. All his years of attempting to stifle whatever existed between him and Lillian were obvious to his mother. He sighed and rose from the table. His mother's scolding could rival any officer's, and he wasn't about to endure more orders.

"I'm going to see John. Believe me, Mum—I won't be seeing her," he said sternly, meaning every single word.

"Fine. Nellie wrote to say she's going to see him tomorrow morning. She can take you."

"You're making Nellie watch me?" he said, walking closer to his door, which he had yet to open. Irritation grew inside him, making his blood boil. First Lillian—now his mother.

"Yes. God knows you can't be trusted where Lillian is concerned."

"You'd be surprised," he said, closing the door. He fell on his bed in full uniform and didn't move all night.

* * *

Morning came quickly, and Samuel rose with more questions than he fell asleep with. He and his mother had left so much unspoken. She always seemed to know more than she said. But somehow, her opinion was always clear.

Samuel splashed his face with the cleanest water he'd seen in months and exited his bare little room. His sister stood in front of him, wearing her own uniform and pulling on her coat.

"I thought you would miss the morning altogether," she teased. He rolled his eyes and hugged her. He had barely seen Nellie at the hospital, and even though the world felt different—being in their home made the night before fade for a moment.

"Pardon me for sleeping. I thought I might rest while I'm home, if you don't mind."

"Well, if you want to see John, it has to be in the morning. He's insufferable in the afternoon, and his leg starts to bother him—what's left of it anyway. He hardly talks to anyone after noon." She spoke factually. The nurturing spirit Nellie had always harbored flew from her mouth and fingertips. Samuel could see why she must love nursing so much—she was good at it. She could earn distinction this way.

The pair of them pulled on their warmer boots and walked on the frozen ground to the Harlow estate. The walk the night before had felt eternal. Samuel wondered how it could seem so short so suddenly. They walked swiftly to the front door, and Samuel watched as Nellie let herself in without even pausing at the door.

"I usually come right in when I'm home. They let me tend to John because I think they assume he'll be kinder to me. They're usually wrong." Nellie must have sensed Samuel's confusion as he walked timidly behind her—perhaps for the first time in his life.

Instead of going up the stairs, Nellie turned down a small hallway past the dining room. Samuel looked in, but not one member of the family had risen yet. Only the servants occupied the familiar room—setting the table and preparing for the day. He couldn't be sure if he was relieved or disappointed by the family's absence. He trotted a few steps to catch up with his sister, who now stood in front of a small wooden door.

"I should warn you—he's not the same at all." And she knocked.

"Go away." John's muffled voice rang from inside.

"Unless there's another nurse in there dressing you, I'm coming in." Nellie walked boldly into the room.

Samuel followed on her heels. His eyes shifted around the door and landed on the youngest Harlow. John's back was to them. A valet and a maid had teamed up to get fresh clothes on his battered body. Samuel could see bruises still fading in places and stitches in the middle of his thigh where the rest of his leg used to extend. John finally pushed himself back onto the bed and almost smiled when he turned to meet Samuel's gaze.

"Well damn, Samuel—took you long enough."

"To what?"

"Come see me. I heard you were here yesterday. Glad to know where I stand. Joking of course, because I can't." John spat each word. Before, a laugh would have come after at least one of his statements, but the corners of his mouth never attempted a smile.

"I'm sorry, John. I didn't know if you were in a position to see me." A lie, of course.

"Well, how do you like the view?" John asked. Nellie shot Samuel an apologetic look. She had warned him—perhaps he should have listened.

"I'm sorry, John. I'm sorry this happened to you."

"No, you're not. You're glad it hasn't happened to you. That's not the same thing."

"John, don't work yourself up. I'll fetch your breakfast," Nellie said—obviously trying to change the subject.

Samuel was happy for her interference, but it was short-lived, since she departed from the room.

The large four-poster where John lay nearly motionless made him look even smaller and more helpless. Samuel sat on the edge of his comrade's bed. John's head turned the other way, revealing a cluster of bruises around his eye and a cut that extended from his jaw to his ear.

"What the hell happened, John?"

"What the hell do you mean? They cut my leg."

"Not that. That," Samuel said, pointing at the left side of John's face.

"Oh. Sliced my face with my blade. Shaving." Samuel didn't believe him, but he didn't want the real answer as much as he thought.

"And the eye?"

"I fell off the bed—not like I could catch myself."

"Nightmares?" Samuel asked.

John's face shifted. His eyes glazed over and stared straight through Samuel.

"I see it all the time. Over and over. It doesn't stop when I'm awake, Samuel. I thought it would stop when I woke up." John spoke frantically—gasping for air with every word.

"What happened, John?" Samuel wanted at least one truth.

"A maid shut my door too hard. Sounded too familiar. I threw myself off the bed but landed on the table there," he said, gesturing to the small stand beside the bed that held a glass of water and a Bible. "Cut my face and gave myself a shiner. Screamed like hell too. They thought I was going to bring the house down." John's eyes glistened, but he didn't let one tear fall.

Samuel had heard of cases like John's. Men who saw the trench even when they had left it, heard the gunshots when they were miles away. No one knew how to help them—any of them—and Samuel knew there would be more like him.

"I get them too," Samuel said. "I saw my friend die. I fall asleep and I see it all again. I see him falling and the blood pouring out. It never stopped." Samuel's words slipped out of his mouth before he knew what they were going to be.

The pair of them jumped when Nellie opened the door holding John's breakfast. She stared at Samuel, looking for some kind of clue in his face as to what went on, but he was sure he looked as ghostly as John did.

"Thank you, Nellie," John said quietly.

Nellie looked stunned—like it was the first time he had ever said it. She laid the tray in front of him and left again, squeezing Samuel's hand as she exited. He was sure she knew she had interrupted something.

"There's one thing I know," John said, shoving a piece of toast into his mouth.

"What's that?" Samuel chuckled lightly at the scene.

"The dead ones are lucky they don't have to see anything anymore." John finished his breakfast and drifted off to sleep. When Nellie returned to collect the empty tray, Samuel finally stood from his place on the side of the bed.

"Nellie, he's terrible," Samuel said, choking on the words.

"He's only half as bad as the others." And then she was gone again, leaving Samuel motionless and alone.

CHAPTER 19

James wandered through the hospital like a ghost. He felt as if he had just seen Samuel, but simultaneously, it felt like a lifetime ago. He had barely seen Samuel when he was home—not that he had expected to. He rarely had time for himself, let alone friends. Even less time for friends who came unannounced in the middle of a war. The single moment Samuel was present at the hospital felt like a dream sequence. One moment he was there, announcing his plans to go home, and the next he was gone like a mirage after the rush of the day. He knew what Samuel would find at his childhood home but had no words to tell him. He had let Samuel return to be surprised—by Lillian and by John. The words in the letter he had received from Lillian indicated Samuel made himself scarce after the initial meeting.

Dear James,

Samuel came here by surprise. You didn't think to call and warn me? I found out he stopped at the hospital before coming here. You truly are despicable. He met Jonah under the worst circumstances. Mother and Father had cornered him in the library. I told him I was engaged. You should have seen how defeated Samuel looked when Jonah walked in the door—like

I had betrayed him somehow. How can that be—when he rejected the feelings I made known to him that day?

I think I want to marry Jonah, but how can I be sure? I was never sure of any of the others. I can't wait for Samuel to feel something for me that he feels he's not allowed to. Am I destined to be alone? With most men dying, can I really risk turning down another man—even if it's not what I want? You're my big brother—tell me what to do. I need someone else's opinion besides Mother's. We obviously know her stance. Please help.

Your sister,
Lillian

He wasn't sure he had ever truly thought his sister would need his help. She always knew her own mind—especially with the men who courted her. Usually, the answer for anything was a resounding *no.* He sat on the only empty cot in the hospital with her letter in his hand and thought about what his answer would be. He would always support Samuel with his sister, but would his parents? Or the rest of society? He had loved him like a brother for so long, but he doubted Samuel would really ever get the chance to be his brother. His thoughts were interrupted when two boots appeared on the floorboards he was staring at.

"James, are you okay?" Nellie asked, plopping down next to him on the cot.

"Yes, I'm okay," he said with a deep sigh. "Lillian's written to me. It seems your brother caused quite a stir."

Nellie looked at the floor and nodded. "Should we have warned him?"

James had wondered the same thing ever since the day of Samuel's return. He had turned around after the bustle of the ambulance arrival, but Samuel was gone, and guilt set in.

"I'm not sure. He might not have gone to the house at all. Lillian wouldn't have forgiven us for it, and maybe it's better he knows."

"I hate seeing him hurt. He's loved her since the first day our father brought us to meet you all. But Jonah is titled, handsome, he clearly understands Lillian—that's a lot for anyone to compete with."

James had never heard Nellie speak so bluntly. She normally protected her brother and his feelings. But in the moment, they agreed.

"Funny how they know each other best but are the least honest with one other." James contemplated his own statement, feeling saddened by the weight of its accuracy. He wished it was easier for both of them. He wished the world was easier for all of them.

"Have you heard from Daniel recently?" Nellie asked. She often kept up on the comings and goings of letters from Daniel, John, or Lillian. But he shook his head.

"No. I haven't heard from him in weeks. Last I knew, he was in France with Samuel. But that was before he came home. I don't know where he is now, but I'm sure he's fine. He was doing so well. He's sure to be a captain in a few months."

He was speaking to Nellie but comforting himself. The letters kept going, but none came back. The fact none had been returned to him was a small comfort. Nellie rose slowly and offered a hand. He took it and pulled himself up—helping her lift his tired body to a standing position.

"Thank you, Nel."

"Don't thank me—I need to clean the cot," she said with a laugh. She moved around him and stripped the stained bedding. The bed smelled like sweat and last night's death, but the smell lingered on the two of them as well, so they had little fear of catching the stench. James exited the room, leaving Nellie to her work, and found two spare pieces of paper. On one, he wrote Lillian and gave his answer.

My dear sister,

I do not believe you are destined to be alone. Quite the contrary. I believe you to have the potential for great love, but what that great love entails is your decision. I believe you could find yourself in love with Captain Winlen if you were to marry him—perhaps you already are. In addition, I believe if he is not the one you choose another man Mother approves of will come along. You have the potential to love him as well. But only potential.

However, we both know you are already in love with Samuel Perry. He might not be what our parents envision. He might not have any money. He might not have the position your other suitors have had. By all accounts, he has nothing. Nothing except everything you need. He doesn't let your stubbornness sway him. He fights you as hard as you fight him. Your friendship has grown exponentially since their first days at our home. I know it is odd for me to speak to you like this, and never have I been called a romantic. God knows my own matters of the heart are muddled and complicated at best. But one thing I have always been sure of—I wish for you to be happy. You are the best of us—without a doubt. And you deserve the best of the world.

I think you have the potential for great happiness. Or you could attempt to seize the happiness you already know you could possess so easily. You must decide which is worth the risk. You could choose the simple, respectable, reasonable choice and risk never loving Captain Winlen the way he and you both deserve. You could risk our parents' disapproval and choose a life with Samuel. But it must be your choice. I cannot tell you what to do this time, as much as I would like to. I can only present you with your true choices. I hope you make the right choice for you, sister. Whatever you decide, I will love you always and support the life you choose.

Your brother,
James

It was perhaps the most sap-filled letter he had ever written, and he almost hated himself for it. Almost. It was true. Every word he wrote came from the sincerest part of himself and bled onto the page. Lillian was perhaps the only person who could invoke words like the ones he wrote. His younger sister—always his ally in childhood—had become his dearest friend in adulthood. He set the letter down beside him and picked up the other paper, but another ambulance raced toward the steps of the hospital.

"Dr. Harlow! There are urgent cases!" Nellie yelled from the room he had left. He always laughed at her professionalism when new men came into the hospital—as if the dying soldiers cared they called each other anything other than Dr. Harlow and Nurse Perry. He pulled on his coverings, stained in so many places they looked dirty even when they had been cleaned.

He strode out of the hospital and met the men at the stairs. He had treated and cleaned up men whose limbs had been severed off. More men followed with blood gushing from their necks and heads. Soldiers were often sent to them with less serious injuries, but as the war had progressed, the doctors in the field simply patched them up to the best of their abilities and saved their lives enough to ship them to established hospitals. James had gotten more troubled cases in the past months than he had gotten at the beginning of the war.

Those bastards sent us dead men. James' frustration with the doctors at the front could not be matched. He was sure of the earnestness of their attempts to save the men they sent home, but with the number of men coming from the trenches—they sent even some of the most serious cases back and to their death. *Proper attention in France or Belgium or wherever they came from could have saved them.* Nellie came up behind him and startled the thoughts out of his mind altogether.

"Nurse Perry," he said quietly, "take the head wound cases to be prepared for operations. All three will need attention. After they are seen to—write their letters home. I am unsure if any of them will make it out of London."

Nellie nodded and ran down the stairs to instruct the men unloading the wounded. James watched the first man carried from the steps, through the hall, and into the small room used as a first-floor operating space. He followed swiftly.

"Name?" he asked, pointing at the unconscious man who lay on the table before him. He was bloodied from hairline to neck and had bandages around his whole head. "What happened to him?"

"Lost his dog tags, but he had a letter on him addressed to a *David*. Shrapnel from a blast. He wasn't caught in it directly, but it cut up his face pretty bad. We don't know if more pieces are in his head. They took out as much as they could when they found him, but he had laid in no-man's-land for hours," the man's carrier said.

James nodded—knowing the severity of the injuries. He removed the bandages that were more red than white. Crimson blood gushed from a hole above his right ear. His hands moved faster than his mind as he saw the sharp, jagged piece of shrapnel stuck only a few centimeters away from the bleed. The extraction was over faster than James even knew he could work, and the blood had finally slowed. However, he had neglected any part of the soldier's face. David's face was bloodied, and his skin had been burned—almost charred—by the blast. James could not bear to remove the bandages and inflict more pain than the man was already feeling.

"Nurse Perry," he called out the door, and Nellie appeared moments later. "This is David. His injuries are severe, but the dangerous shrapnel has been removed. The injuries on his face will surely be the most painful for him and might keep him unconscious longer than we would hope. If he wakes up, make sure you take down a letter to his loved ones. We cannot be sure he will come through it, and even if he does, he most definitely will not look the same. Better to prepare his family."

They were orders he had given a million times, but each word felt painful even to him. He hated the letters home from the hospital. They so rarely meant the soldiers would be coming home at all, or if they did, the letters were only a warning for what was to come. Dr. Walker approached to relieve him of his duties after the intricacy of the operation he had just performed.

"Dr. Harlow, let me take over. Go home. Sleep. I will call you back in the morning."

Normally, he would argue with the instructions, but when he counted the hours in his head since he last slept, he could not. He exited and flung off the coverings that had added a new stain to the collection. Grabbing the paper he had stuffed in his pockets when the ambulance arrived, he penned one last letter before staggering home in the hazy night.

Daniel,

I have not heard from you in weeks. This is a final effort to reach you before worry truly sets in. I know we have had our differences, our resentments, and our quarrels, but this war has made every last one seem silly and useless. The inheritance, the estate, the women we fought over, our father's approval, our mother's affection—none of it seems to matter anymore. We could not have been more stupid than to envy each other for things neither of us could control or change. I watch men younger than us die in front of me every day, and I almost envy their ability to serve while I am stuck here, forced to witness their decline despite my efforts. Always one step behind, it seems. Please send word when you receive this. Say hello to Samuel for me—last I knew, you two were together in France. I hope to be reunited with you both soon.

Your brother,
James

CHAPTER 20

James had only been asleep for five hours when he was called back to the hospital. He was grateful, however, for any sleep he was granted. He pulled his clothes back on and stepped out into the cold January wind. The world thought the war would never last into the harshness of winter, but instead it simply added to it. Snow had started to fall, and James pulled his coat over his ears to protect them from the flurries and climbed the hospital stairs carefully. Inside, the icy nature of the day was only an extension of the frigid outside.

He strode through the door, ready for whatever new injuries he would face. Nellie stood waiting for him in the room where they took a break on a cot the day before. He could never read her face accurately, because she, like every other doctor and nurse, learned how to stay neutral for the sake of the soldiers around them. Each day, their faces had to hide the knowledge of the severity of each wound.

"James, we called you back about the man with shrapnel wounds."

"David? Does he need another surgery? Is that why I was called back?"

"Yes, he needs another surgery," she started. "He's critical, but you can't perform it."

“What do you mean? I started on him, and I know what’s already been done. I am best equipped to handle whatever he needs.”

Bloody Walker. Always stealing my surgeries after I do the worst, and he gets all the glory. Must be nice being the head doctor. He turned to go back to the operating table.

Nellie yelled after him. “James! You can’t!”

He whipped around. “Why the bloody hell not, Nellie?”

“Because his name isn’t David! It’s Daniel.”

James stood stunned and confused at the words. His brother’s name came from her mouth, but he could not understand her meaning, no matter how many times he tried.

“I don’t understand. They said his name was David when they brought him in. They said there was a letter addressed to a David.” He stumbled in between each sentence and rolled into the next statement. He pulled anything from his memory that could prove her wrong.

“He didn’t have any other identification on him, so they used the letter,” Nellie said. “But it was smeared from the elements. They guessed it said David. It was one of your letters to Daniel. It’s him. I found out not even an hour ago. You asked me to get his information and draft a letter when he woke up. He was asleep for hours until he finally woke. He was confused. I asked him where to send a letter to, and he said, “Frederick and Mary Harlow.” He said my name. He asked for you, and he was unconscious again. They think he may have a hemorrhage.”

James listened in a daze. He had operated on his own brother. His elder brother had lain on the table in front of him, and James had worn his blood only hours before. He stumbled away from Nellie and landed almost on top of one of the men behind him. Nellie rushed to steady him and supported his steps to a chair in the back corner of the hospital. His mind raced, but at the same time, it understood nothing at all.

"How long has he been unconscious?" he asked, fearing the answer.

"He passed out about forty minutes ago. Dr. Walker took him in immediately. I haven't seen him since. I was instructed to tell you. I think they assumed it would help, coming from a friend."

James nodded—unsure of what else to do. He found his feet again and walked to the door he knew his brother lay behind and slid down to the floor like he had the day they both went to enlist. He hadn't smoked since the war started on account of the men he treated and their already compromised lungs, but he wished for nothing more than a cigarette. His head hit the old, tattered door with a bang he knew they could hear. It was his small attempt to let his brother know he was there, even if Daniel never heard the thud.

"Nel?" he whispered. She had not moved from where she stood only a handful of steps away. He felt her eyes on him, so he knew the whisper would be received even in the quietest tone. "Go in for me. Make sure they do everything." He looked up at her—refusing to accept the truth that sat like a demon next to him.

She nodded and slipped around him. When she opened the door, James saw his brother with blood under his head. Electric shocks were being transmitted into his already weakening body with the hope one would jolt him awake. Then, for perhaps the first time since the war started, James begged God to spare just one soldier.

* * *

James sat by the door for over two hours. No one bothered him. Each staff member knew the circumstances and not one even approached him. He had managed to bum a cigarette off a soldier in the cot closest to him, but even he knew not to ask James why he sat on the floor of the hospital. The door opened behind him suddenly and almost flung him backward into the room. He scrambled to his feet as Dr. Walker emerged with Nellie close behind him. They stood silent, and James stared at the top of his brother's head as he lay on the table behind the door.

Nellie shook her head and looked at the floor. Dr. Walker was the first one to speak.

"Dr. Harlow," he started. "Your brother suffered a severe hemorrhage of the brain. After the injuries he sustained, we were unable to help him further. He's gone."

James shook his head and looked at him squarely—moving his gaze from Daniel.

"You bastard," he spat.

"Dr. Harlow—"

"You complete bastard! I could have saved him. I took shrapnel from his head. I stopped the bleeding myself. I did that! You didn't call me until he was already in the room! You should have let me in, and you know it!" He had hardly raised his voice to another human being his whole life, but his agony rang clearly and could certainly be heard throughout the hospital.

Nellie crossed Dr. Walker and faced James, blocking further insults. "Dr. Harlow, you may go in to say your goodbyes."

She said it so sweetly, but he knew it was not a request. He moved around her, glaring at the doctor, and slammed the door behind him. The room was lit only by the morning light coming in. January had been so dull, it seemed almost cruel the sun appeared the same day Daniel ceased to exist. James stood over his brother's body, unsure of what to say or do. Without even knowing why, he began to speak.

"You're a bastard too, you know." He half-laughed, trying to make the moment lighter somehow. "This is some kind of trick. I always wanted the estate, the money, the approval of the great Frederick Harlow, and you never did. Now look at you—giving it to me on accident. You prig."

Tears flowed, but James' voice never faltered. Instead, he continued and let the tears drop onto his brother's bloody shoulder.

"John lost a leg. You idiots couldn't have been more careful? Lillian's trying to decide what to do about Samuel. Oh right, you didn't know about that. Well, Lillian loves our gardener. Mother would love that if she knew, wouldn't she?" He laughed truly this time and wiped his sleeve across his face and let it absorb any and all moisture. "I'm jealous of you, you know. You got all the girls. You were the firstborn. You traveled more than I was ever able to. You got to serve and I didn't. Even now, I'm jealous of you, I think. Because you get to rest and die a hero while I have to stay here and do the job I know was never meant for me. I have to try and fix everything now that you're gone. I don't really think I could have saved you. I'm so sorry . . ." His voice finally stilled. It had grown quieter the longer the speech went on, but suddenly, nothing else came.

James collapsed. Nellie rushed in, having heard the crash of the metal supplies James knocked over. They were still covered in the eldest Harlow's blood. He sat on the floor with silent screams erupting from his heart while Nellie reached out to help him stand. He clutched her hand and stayed in his position of grief on the seedy floor of the London hospital.

Finally, he rose slowly, his hand climbing up Nellie's arm as she steadied him. His vision was blurred from the tears, and the finality filling the room left him exhausted and heavy.

"Dr. Walker gave you the day off. You can go back to your flat and rest," Nellie said, but James shook his head.

"No. I'll stay. I have work to do, and there are bound to be more ambulances today."

"James, I don't think—"

"I have to do something," he interrupted. "I can't go back to my empty flat, and I can't let someone else's brother die today. Even if Walker can."

And he left her standing with Daniel's body. He pulled on his coverings, walked out into the January sunshine, and let the cold flurries land on him—hoping they would cleanse the feeling of the day from him, but he had a distinct feeling he would never wash it away. He lifted his head to meet the sky, and each flake that touched his face woke him to the work he had yet to do and the days of death he knew had just begun. Nellie appeared beside him and stood with him in silence. Neither one moved nor spoke, but James heard every sympathy his friend's heart whispered. He felt her shiver, and he turned to go back inside—facing her first.

"Thank you." He could say only that, but he knew she understood. She nodded, and as he left her to make his rounds, he finally heard Nellie Perry break.

CHAPTER 21

Lillian sat quietly in her dark and empty home. She couldn't remember the last time she had been in proper mourning. Most likely for a distant relative she hadn't met more than a few times. Never for anyone she loved as much as her brother. When James wrote with the news about Daniel, her mother went numb. Silently, Lillian watched her pull out every article of black clothing in the house.

"These all need to be altered and mended before we go out again," she said. Lillian had yet to see her cry. She had wished so many times for her mother to stop talking. Now more than ever, Lillian wished she would say something—anything.

How strange grief is. One emotion, so well known, sits so different in each person's heart, she thought.

Lillian walked down the stairs slowly and followed the corridor to the room of the house John now occupied. She entered without knocking and met a groggy, half-asleep Harlow. She noticed streaks on his face where tears had flowed but thought it best not to bring attention to them. She hadn't even seen John cry for his own misfortune, but somehow she knew everyone in the house would weep for Daniel.

She crossed to fidget with the window drapes cautiously—not wanting to endure the wrath John had been frequently giving all who entered.

"What are you doing here, Lillian?" he asked in his usual ugly tone.

She circled the room and plopped onto the chaise longue at the foot of his bed. She lay her arms on the covers and let her head rest on top. The two sat quietly together—which seemed more important this time. John stared at her. Clearly, he was waiting for a response.

"I just—didn't want to be alone," she said quietly.

"It should've been me," he said, turning to stare at the wall instead of meeting her eyes.

"It shouldn't have been any of you," she answered.

"He was so smart. How could he have been stupid enough to let this happen?" John's voice grew louder and tears streamed from his eyes again.

Lillian reached for his whole leg. Her hand rested on his ankle until John finally turned back to face her. She breathed deeply—finding strength from the bottom of her soul.

"No one can know why this happened, John. No one can understand why. God knows I don't."

"Why am I like this? Why is Daniel dead? What the hell is happening, Lily? This wasn't supposed to happen!" John fell into hysterics. Lillian rose quickly and moved to sit on the bed next to her brother. She cradled him like a child and searched for the right words.

This was the only time she had considered John's injury to be a strange blessing. It hindered his ability to escape the family or his own feelings. Now he was forced to sit in it—and she sat with him—missing Daniel and their lives before the war.

"I don't know why any of this is happening, John. I don't have an answer. Just because I'm older than you doesn't mean I understand any more than you," she said, finally releasing him. She watched him wipe his sleeve across his face to make any and all tears disappear.

I don't even understand my own heart, she thought.

Her concentration was broken by her mother entering the room. She hardly ever visited John, so Lillian knew she had to be coming for her. John must have known as well, because he turned on his side and closed his eyes—preparing to sleep again.

"What, Mother?" Lillian asked indignantly. She stood up from the bed and crossed the room to her mother—attempting to usher her from the room.

"You have a visitor," her mother said plainly, without feeling and unmoving.

Lillian sped past her—wanting nothing more than his comforting arms. She wasn't sure how he had managed leave again, but she didn't care. He came. She ran around the corner and checked the library but found it empty. She scanned the empty foyer and caught Mr. Taylor by the front door.

"Where is he?" she almost screamed.

Mr. Taylor pointed, and she followed his finger out the front door. She stopped dead in her tracks when she came face-to-face with her guest.

"Lily," Jonah said, rushing toward her. "I'm so sorry. I was sent to London. I went to see James at the hospital before coming here. The Perry girl—Nellie—she told me what happened. I sent telegrams to my superiors. I'm here for whatever you need through the funeral. It's in a few days, I assume?"

Lily nodded and accepted the embrace he offered. He said all the right things, sped to her side, offered to stay—most likely risking disciplinary action to do so, and none of it mattered.

In that moment, she knew. The man she was racing toward in her grief wasn't Jonah.

It was Samuel.

And she wept. Her tears fell partly for her brother and partly because the wrong man stood in front of her, and she knew it more than ever.

* * *

Jonah remained just like he said he would. Lillian was grateful for his company, but each moment they spent together filled her with guilt and regret. From helping with the flower arrangements her mother couldn't finish to talking with her father who now had to entrust the estate to James. Every moment Jonah was at her side, and she hated herself for it.

She asked for as much time alone as she could without drawing suspicion from him or her mother. She wasn't positive Mary Harlow would return to reality, but she wouldn't let her altered feelings for Jonah be the thing that brought her back. Her moments of isolation did not contain any comfort.

She found herself in her room wondering how she could tell a perfect angel of a man she couldn't marry him. She couldn't bring herself to write to James—not that she thought he would answer anyway. If she knew her brother at all, he was either drinking himself into oblivion or working relentlessly until the funeral.

So she did the only thing she knew how—she wrote to Samuel.

Dear Samuel,

You won't ever see this letter. It will go in a drawer or burn the second I finish. But I need to write it—to say it again in something addressed to you. Just once.

I'm not marrying Jonah. He doesn't know yet. I can't. I knew it a few days ago when I wished you were here in his place.

I love you. I didn't say it that day at the train because I was too afraid to say the whole truth when you had already told me no. You were probably right—and I wish you weren't.

I wish I could love someone else but you. But I'm almost certain I never will. How unfair.

Daniel died. James is terrible. I've just learned the course of my own heart. John lost his leg and himself. Nellie can never unsee the horrors she's witnessed. And you—you're still out there somewhere fighting. How unfair. All of it.

I love you. I'm sorry I do.

All my love, always,
Lillian

She sealed the letter completely, let her candle share its flames, threw it into her fireplace, and watched her confession burn.

CHAPTER 22

Samuel's disposition had not improved since leaving the Harlow estate and Lillian. If anything, it had worsened since winter had come to the trenches. He had only gone to the estate to see John. The poor boy had turned thin and fragile both in body and mind. He had heard about the condition of some returning men, but witnessing it in a boy he had tried to look after his whole life was another matter entirely. Samuel knew little about the ailment, but he knew more news of the war would not help him in any way. He tried so hard to forget about Lillian and Captain Winlen. Lillian was engaged, and Captain Winlen looked at her like she was everything. Samuel had looked at her the same way.

The mornings in the trenches were almost bearable, but waiting in the winter was more tortuous than waiting any other time of the year. The season itself almost demanded waiting. The nights were agonizingly cold and raids meant traveling into the blustery and unprotected land outside the trench. Overall, Samuel returned to the trenches and found them different—just like they found him different. His thoughts of the Harlows and his own family seemed to fill his mind even more than before.

Strange, how I thought she would be waiting for me. He wondered how he ever thought that life, or Mrs. Harlow, would stop when he went off to war. She had been flinging men at Lillian since she was of age, and Samuel was stuck watching. But never once did he think one would actually charm her and turn her head. Samuel's thoughts fled from his mind when Albert approached him.

"Perry, you've been somewhere else since your leave ended. What happened with that girl?"

If it was possible, Albert's subtlety had depleted even more than his tact.

"Nothing happened. I surprised her—just like I planned." It was true. He had surprised her, but she had surprised him too that day.

"And?"

"And another man was there—a captain. Captain Winlen. They're engaged. She's been writing to him—I didn't even know she had someone else."

Albert looked at him and rolled his eyes. "She's been writing you too, Sam. You've gotten more letters from this woman you claim is your friend than some married men have gotten."

He knew it was true. Albert seemed oddly invested in his relationship, but somehow his words sank in.

"She all but told me she loved me the day I left for training. She came to the train station to tell me, and I told her nothing could happen. I mean, I'm her gardener for God's sake. What kind of life would she have? Society would never accept her again, and I would lose the best and only position I've ever had. Lieutenant Harlow, the man who came here and knew me, that's her brother. He said the world wouldn't be the same when the war is over, and I believed him. So I went to see her—to see if she might believe it. But I met the captain instead." Samuel felt the disdain in his voice when he said the word *captain*. Admitting he was hurt was far harder than allowing anger to fill his voice.

"So you love her. Right?" Albert asked.

Samuel laughed. If the other men heard the subject of their conversation, they would be brutally mocked. It definitely wasn't the usual talk that went on in the trenches when it came to women. He looked at Albert, who lit two cigarettes and handed one to Samuel—waiting for his answer.

"Yeah, I do." He had never admitted it out loud, and only rarely to himself. It felt odd to say it in a war zone, but it flowed from his mouth naturally and without a hint of fear.

"Then forget about the excuses you're pretending matter and tell her," Albert said, and he rose—ready to leave.

"But they do matter. Don't they?" Samuel asked.

"They didn't matter to her when she told you, did they? Wasn't she risking just as much as you—if not more? You need to decide if it's worth it. And then you can stop moping around. Because in case you haven't noticed, we're at war. It's depressing enough without you worrying about a girl."

Samuel smirked. Clearly Albert was done with sentimentality for the day, and he left Samuel alone with his thoughts.

Samuel took the box of Lillian's letters and set it in front of him. The hair ribbon was losing its color, and the perfume had faded enough for Samuel to barely remember it. It wrapped around the stack of letters that felt larger than he remembered and the book pages Lillian had sent with him to war. Each one had become a little tattered around the edges, and he shook his head, laughing again at her ability to tear a page from a book. He dropped the parcel when he was startled by a familiar voice.

"Perry, mail."

Samuel leapt up and stopped the man. "What's your name?"

The man halted abruptly, then smiled. "No one ever asks," he said. "It's Henry."

"Hello, Henry. Thank you for always bringing our letters. I'm Samuel." He extended his hand, and Henry shook it.

The smile widened across the wartime postman's face, and he left, continuing on his way.

Samuel examined the letter Henry had delivered. There was only one—from James. He set it aside and considered his conversation with Albert.

He knew if Mary Harlow decided Lillian's future, he would never be in it. While he was sure of the respect and affections of Frederick and Mary Harlow, he was also sure he was not what they wanted for their only daughter. The way he was ushered away on his leave to avoid seeing Lillian proved it.

His own mother had forbidden him from facing Lillian again when he was home—not that he had wanted to. Nellie would support him—he knew that. Daniel and James could almost certainly be counted on—he knew that too. But would that be enough for her? He couldn't be sure any declaration would matter anymore. She had a fiancé with more than he could ever offer her, but suddenly—it didn't matter.

He reached for the stack of book pages and found the one Lillian had torn from *Emma*. Regardless of whether the page she chose to gift him was intentional or not, it was the one he needed to send. He searched for his pen and underlined one line. It belonged to Knightley—the man Lillian had once compared to him.

"If I loved you less, I might be able to talk about it more."

He hadn't been able to comprehend the meaning of the line when he read the words aloud in his younger days, but in that moment, sitting in a hole in the ground, he understood every word. And what words could be better? So he signed his name and sealed it in an envelope—ready to tell her for the first time. When he thought of what telling her meant, bliss finally filled him instead of dread.

He turned to James' letter and tore it open—his heart still pounding.

Samuel,

I wish I was writing to you with better news. Daniel was wounded and needed shrapnel removed from his head as well as mending other injuries. His head was in bad shape, and he suffered a hemorrhage. He's dead.

I wish I could see you to tell you this news, but preparations are being made for the funeral, and I wanted it to reach you in time. Seeing as you were just home on leave, and I can't be sure when this letter will reach you—I'm sure returning home will be close to impossible. But if you are at all able to come, you'd be more than welcome at the services on January 16.

I don't know when you saw him last, but know he was fond of you, like we all are. Please stay safe. We are all devastated, and I'm sure we could not sustain another loss.

James

Samuel sat stunned. The joy he'd felt from preparing Lillian's letter disappeared with the news of Daniel's death. James' letter was factual—void of most emotion. With Daniel's death, James would receive the estate, the inheritance, everything. Except now, it would be impossible to live with, knowing Daniel had to die for it.

His grief sank into his chest until his breath came in fast, shallow gasps. Suddenly, he saw George falling on the barbed wire all over again. Except now, Daniel lay by his side. The visions flashed in his mind until he had to physically shake his head to get them to leave. They wouldn't stay away for long.

Suddenly, Henry returned. "Perry, you okay?"

Samuel nodded but said nothing. He handed him the envelope for Lillian and sat down slowly, still trying to digest the news from James.

Henry took the letter but didn't ask anything further. He turned away and shuffled a stack of letters in his hand for the men down the trench. Samuel watched him turn once more and approach again. "Perry, I overlooked this one. You have another letter. Looks like orders."

Samuel took the letter slowly and dreaded the contents. After the news of Daniel, he wasn't sure what else he would be able to take.

With the great need for military officers and the examination of your skills, you, Samuel Arthur Perry, have been promoted to the rank of second lieutenant. Report to your commanding officer in three days to receive your orders. The German army progresses on the Western Front near Champagne. You will be allowed twenty-four hours leave on January 21 beginning at 0900 hours to prepare. You will then remain in Champagne until further notice.

One day.

Samuel had one day to return home. Even though it would be after Daniel's funeral, he knew he had to go. He had to go home.

CHAPTER 23

Lillian pinned her black hat onto her head and let the small veil fall over her eyes. She had pulled her hair up neatly so not a single piece fell. Of all the days to showcase her usual subtle defiance—her brother's funeral was certainly not one. Her black dress fell over her shoulders, making her pale skin look even lighter than usual. She moved to her bedside table where she picked up her engagement ring. She pushed it onto her finger. Once, it had felt like a perfect fit, but now it strangled her hand and seemed to weigh more than she did, choking her slowly. She pulled her gloves on—forcing the left one over the stone—and strode out of her room into the most terrible day she could recall.

Jonah stood in uniform, waiting for her at the bottom of the stairs like he had on Christmas Eve. He offered his arm when she finally descended the staircase. She took it with reluctance, but she also couldn't bear any more heartache than what the Harlow family already bore. She and Jonah walked behind her parents while James staggered behind. He still smelled of alcohol, and not one bit of it was expensive—of that she was certain. He looked as if he hadn't properly slept in days. Nellie came from behind—pushing John in a wheelchair over the frozen ground. His lack of leg was on display for the first time, as one leg of his trousers hung limp.

Lillian was sure he would make Nellie stay as far behind as he could.

The day was bitterly cold, and the harsh wind made the veil on Lillian's hat swirl and hit her eyes repeatedly. She clung to Jonah's arm—mostly for warmth and obligation rather than affection.

The Harlow family plot held numerous relatives who had died in the last century and a half at least, and now Daniel would join them. Lillian gazed into a small plot—her brother's final resting place. The headstone wouldn't be added until spring, but she wondered if it would really ever feel real. In a way, she hoped it wouldn't. Believing it to be a terrible dream for the rest of her life somehow felt more bearable.

She knew her father had told all involved to keep the service brief. Lillian looked at her mother—it was surely for her benefit. She knew Daniel's death couldn't be discussed in front of her for long. The entire family had been waiting for the lady of the house to break every day since the news arrived.

The service began with words of prayer, requests to give the family peace and praises for how honorably Daniel served. Lillian didn't listen to a word. She stared into the ground and wished for it not to be true. Lillian felt Jonah squeeze her hand softly as her tears fell.

She watched him standing tall, motionless, and serene. He looked straight ahead, showing no weakness, but she knew his large heart behind the uniform. He was steady, safe, kind—and she didn't want him. It made no sense, but she cried harder and looked away from him.

"Amen," the rest of her family mumbled. Her father's pleas for a short service must have worked. She never heard the message and ignored the prayer completely. She was sure so many of the prayers she had said in the past days were similar to the one she missed. Many more would follow in the coming days.

Her family slipped away one by one, beginning with Nellie wheeling John away. Her father led her mother away slowly and left James and Jonah alone with her. James stepped closer and pulled a flask from his coat. He took a big gulp and swallowed hard.

"Funny, isn't it?" James began.

Lillian turned to face her brother. "What?"

"I got everything I ever wanted, and now I don't want it at all. Bloody ironic." He gulped once more, laughing sadly. He moved to kiss her on the cheek and shake Jonah's hand. Lillian watched him stumble after the rest of the family, leaving her alone with her fiancé. Jonah began to lead her away from the gravesite, but she pulled back her hand and walked toward a familiar name.

"We should be going, Lillian. It's been a long day already, and it's much too cold out here," Jonah said, shadowing her.

"In a minute. I just wanted to say hello," she said, eyeing the stone.

"William Perry. As in—" Jonah started.

"Private Perry's father. Yes," she interrupted. She could hear Jonah's deep breath beside her, and suddenly, she knew. She couldn't stand it another minute.

"Jonah—"

"Don't," he stopped her.

"Don't what?"

"Don't do whatever you're about to do or say. Whatever you think I should hear. I assure you—I don't want to hear it, and I promise our lives will be wonderful if you don't. So please don't."

She took a deep breath and let all the words fall out with one exhale. "Jonah, I can't marry you."

"You can. I could make you happy," he said it simply. She knew he believed it. He wasn't begging her—he was telling her.

"Perhaps. But I couldn't make you as happy as you deserve to be. Not when I can't love you the right way." Lillian turned away from her former gardener's grave and paced nervously. Her boots slammed the hard ground, making a sound that matched the thumping in her chest.

"How long have you known?" he asked—turning to face her.

"Known what?"

"That you wouldn't marry me. Did you ever even want to? Did you mean it when you said yes?" The questions caused her as much pain to hear as they must have caused him to ask.

"I did. I thought I did. But when you came, Mother said I had a visitor, and I—"

"—didn't want it to be me," he finished for her.

Silence.

Lillian shuffled toward him slowly and stopped over a foot away, but a ravine seemed to gape between them. She pulled her black glove off her left hand and turned her engagement ring around her finger once before finally removing it altogether. She held it carefully in her hands—staring at it before looking up at Jonah.

"I love you. I do," she said, moving closer and putting the ring in Jonah's palm. She watched him fiddle with the small band and large stone as she had.

"But you're not in love with me?" he asked. Lillian slowly shook her head and let her tears fall for a second time. Jonah nodded and bent down slowly to kiss her cheek but stopped inches from it. She turned her head and met his gaze, but he stood slowly and turned—walking away from her.

"Does he know you're in love with him?" he yelled from steps away.

She stood stunned. "He does."

She watched Jonah match her surprise. She wasn't sure if he was surprised she had answered, she understood the question, or she had answered it honestly.

"I knew too, you know. You looked at him like you had waited all your life for him to walk through that door for you," he said with a sad smile.

"I have." For the first time, she couldn't care less someone besides James knew. Nothing would change, but she wouldn't deny it any longer. She couldn't.

Jonah nodded slowly. "Goodbye, Miss Harlow."

"Goodbye, Captain Winlen." And she turned away from him to face the grave of Samuel's father once again as Jonah's footsteps grew fainter.

She stood completely alone in the cold and smiled.

Loneliness and sadness tugged at her heart, but she was free.

CHAPTER 24

Samuel wasted no time the morning of his short, one day leave. It was no time at all, but also all he needed. He had wished for word from Lillian before returning but had received none. Even with his desire to see her, he truly only wanted to see his mother and be in his own home for a few short hours before being damned to the trenches for however long the war lasted. He took nothing with him except his box of letters—refusing to leave it.

"Private!" Albert yelled from down the trench.

"That's Second Lieutenant to you, Blake," Samuel replied with a smile, which resulted in a salute from his comrade.

"Make sure you come back," he said with mischief in his eyes. Samuel laughed at Albert's desertion joke. He gave a nod to his friend and turned to go.

The sun had decided to hide away on the cold January day. Samuel arrived at the docks, wondering if the boat would even make the journey across the Channel without plowing into an iceberg like *Titanic*. He leaned over the railing, as if his will would make them reach England sooner. The spray of the water washed away the emotions of the past days, and he thought only of the few hours he had at home. The ride seemed endless, but Samuel finally docked and raced to the train that would take him back to Staffordshire.

The train brought him to the station at almost three o'clock in the afternoon. Samuel marveled at how little time he already had left after five hours of travel home. He walked from the station down the familiar streets until he reached the doorstep of his own home. He strode in the door like he had when he was last on leave and was met by his mother mending a dress at the small kitchen table. His mother jumped up from her chair and ran to him.

"Samuel Arthur Perry! You have to stop surprising us like this!" And she slapped his shoulder but hugged him tightly until Samuel had to force her release. He watched his mother scan him. He stood tall in his long, straight coat and second lieutenant's hat. His mother made him a cup of tea and laid it down at his place, which he was sure had remained empty as long as he had been away.

Samuel sat at his place, tea in hand, and smiled. "Mum, I have something to tell you."

Anna Perry looked down at him as she poured more water in his barely emptied cup. "Yes?"

"I got promoted. I'm a second lieutenant." He smiled.

Anna Perry dropped the kettle on the table, almost spilling the remainder of the water. She lowered herself to his level and held his face in her hands before kissing the top of his head. "Your father would be so proud of you."

Samuel sat quietly content. It was the first time she had mentioned their father without tears or a silent moment after. Instead, it now flowed naturally—like she could one day talk about him again.

"I haven't told the Harlows I've come either." He sipped his tea and received another slap from his mother, which made him spill the hot drink down himself.

"You know what happened last time, you daft boy."

"I didn't have time to write to anyone this time. I got my promotion, my orders, and my leave so quickly. I had no time to warn you. I need to go back to see her. I need to apologize for how I acted when I was last home. To ask her—" He stopped. "Well, either way, I came to see you all. I can't know when I'll get the opportunity again." He spoke plainly. Even when he had tried to change the subject, his mother watched him with suspicion but said nothing further. He grew tired of hiding his feelings, but his mother had made her feelings clear about him staying away. But he couldn't—not without making sure she knew, at least once, before marrying the captain.

He and his mother talked through their tea about Nellie, his promotion, and the war until Anna Perry rose and announced she had to collect a mending project from a neighbor down the street. Samuel watched his mother bundle herself in his father's old coat and a scarf Nellie had made for her years ago and disappear into the cold evening air.

Samuel wandered the rooms of his home alone, feeling out of place. It looked like his home, but each time he returned, he felt more different than the last, and his home felt less and less familiar. He sat on his bed in his empty room and enjoyed the space the same way he had before he left. So much had changed since the morning he left for training. His front door opened suddenly and closed with a bang.

"Mum?"

"Sammy?" His sister's voice rang out, and the tone demanded an explanation.

"What are you doing here?" he asked, walking to the kitchen once again. He found his sister removing her worn coat and gloves. She smiled at him, but moved toward him quickly.

"Never mind that. You're supposed to be in France, you idiot," she said as she punched his arm.

"You and Mum really have to stop hitting me."

"Well, if you'd start telling us when you were coming," she said with a smile. "I came home to have dinner with Mum."

She took off her coat and began cooking. Samuel watched his efficient little sister and remained as stunned as ever. She prepared their mother's shepherd's pie, which happened to be one of his favorites. He smiled and sat at the table behind her.

"Were you there? When he died?" Samuel asked. Nellie breathed in and slowly stepped back from her preparations.

"I was. It was terrible. We didn't know it was him at first. We found out. James was monstrous with the other doctors, but he's getting better. It helps we constantly have work to do, I suppose," she said, turning back to the meal.

Before Samuel had time to ask more questions, his mother returned with the mending in hand. She smiled at both of her children, and Samuel grinned—thankful for a moment with the two of them together again. The news of Daniel made him feel increasingly mortal, and a minute of happiness was a gift.

It didn't last long enough. Dinner was served, eaten, and cleaned up within a few hours, and Samuel watched the time like it was his greatest enemy. He stood, and both his mother and sister looked up at him knowingly.

"It's seven o'clock. I have something to do before I go. I have to go now if I want to catch the last train at ten o'clock. I'll catch the last boat back to France out of London." He looked down at his sister, who smiled at him like she knew something. But she never said a word.

Nellie stood first and hugged her brother, then made room for their mother—only moving over a few inches. The three of them stood in an embrace. Samuel's head rested on the top of theirs, and they stayed in the kitchen, unmoving for a minute until their mother spoke.

"Well, go on then. Be safe."

He nodded, leaned down, and kissed her cheek. He pecked Nellie's head and exited. He glanced at the familiar lane and headed for the Harlow home.

* * *

Samuel walked down the familiar lane feeling like he carried his emotions in his hands—waiting for them to be smashed. He had sent the page, readied himself to return home, but had never considered what he would say to his friend past "I'm sorry." He agonized over the upcoming conversation, wondering how he could manage to put eleven years of stolen glances, accidental touches, friendly laughs, and almost somethings into what she deserved to hear. He finally made it to the Harlow estate, but before attempting to go to the house, his feet carried him to the end of his familiar route—to the greenhouse. It was cold and the windows had frosted, but somehow stepping inside made him feel warm again. He let his pack thump beside an empty pot and wandered inside his home away from home. Amazingly, it was the only place that felt completely unchanged.

He sat on one of the empty benches and took out the stack of letters he had brought with him. He turned them over in his hands, and some of the ink came off on his fingers. Somehow, Lillian's words bleeding onto his hands was comforting. He held them tightly and allowed his eyes to close. He listened to the greatly missed sound of near-silence and was grateful for each moment of it.

When he knew too much time had passed, he stood and readied himself to go to the house, still unsure of what words would come out of his mouth. He grabbed his pack, looking once more at the resting flowers, and hoped he would see them in the spring again. He left the greenhouse, but his bag slipped from his grip once more when he looked toward the familiar hill and saw her.

Lillian was dressed in a cream-colored shirt with a lacy collar that wove halfway up her neck and a deep blue skirt and coat. Her hat had clearly been thrown on rather than pinned correctly, and her hair had started to come undone and lay around her shoulders. He walked up behind her, not making a sound until he was only a few feet behind her.

"Hello, stranger."

Lillian whipped around at the sound of his voice. She looked him up and down—confused but smiling.

"You again," she said, breath shooting out of her mouth in the cold January weather. "You came back."

"I came back. I only have one day—most of which I've already spent at home, but I had to see you. I had to apologize for how I acted."

She stepped toward him down the hill and hesitated before speaking. "You came all the way from France for one day?"

"Yes. I'm sorry, Lily. When I came home last, I wasn't expecting you to be—well, for there to be someone else. Not that there wasn't supposed to be someone else. I just—I wasn't expecting you to have—"

"For me to have met someone else?" she said, stopping his rambling.

"Yes," he started. He walked past her until he reached the top of the hill. He turned slowly. "Lillian, I sent you something after I heard the news about Daniel. I can't be sure you've gotten it. But the last time I saw Daniel, he told me things wouldn't be the same once the war ends. I think he was right. But mostly because I don't want things to be the same. Because what I want is what you wanted the day I left. It's what I've always wanted."

He watched Lillian open the small bag she held and pull out the single book page that had traveled to France and back.

She stepped toward him until she was only a pace from him. "Did you mean it, or do you just hate the idea of me with someone else?"

"I most definitely hate the idea of you with someone else," he said with a grin. "I have since the day we stole that damn book. I mean it." He stood quietly, unsure if his words would make any difference.

"I'm not engaged."

Samuel's head whipped up. "You're not—? But when?"

"After Daniel died, he came. He was here, and he was lovely and wonderfully kind, but when he arrived, I realized the only person I wanted in that moment—was you."

Samuel took one small step, filling the gap and putting a gloved hand on her waist—somewhere it had never been before. The movement made her head jerk and pause a mere inch from his own. He leaned down and found the courage not only to risk the life he had but to seize the life he wanted. He felt her stand taller in his arms. When her lips fell into his, he wondered how he had ever been without them.

Her feet touched the ground again, and he smiled at her. "You just had to kiss me first, didn't you?"

"Well, it seemed only right. You made me wait all this time, you weasel." She giggled.

"Weasel? You once said you'd never love a weasel of a man," he teased.

"I remember." She nodded—her eyes twinkling back at him.

"Do you think you could marry one?" he said, kneeling in his uniform, removing his hat, and letting it fall to the ground. "I love you, Lily. I have for so long. I can't promise you money or a title, but I can guarantee what you asked for that day. I can guarantee a lifetime of knowing each other."

Lillian's face went from joking to pure shock, landing somewhere joyful. She filled the space between them, tackling him, and he kissed her again.

"I don't know when it could be," he said. "I doubt I'll be home anytime soon, and God knows how long this damn war will last, but—"

"Oh stop, Sam. Yes. Yes, whenever you come back to me—I'll marry you." She sat up, allowing him up as well. The cold ground had soaked into his uniform, but he didn't feel a thing.

"Oh, God, Lily what's the time? I have to make the last train."

Samuel stood, reached for his hat, and helped Lillian to her feet. He ran down the hill to his pack. He flung it over his shoulder with one hand and grabbed her hand with the other. He ran with her to the front of the house, and she ordered the car from Mr. Taylor. He climbed in quickly and began to close the door, but Lillian's gloved hand stopped him.

"Oh no you don't, Samuel Perry. I'm not letting you out of my sight until I have to." She climbed in after him.

The car drove faster than Samuel knew it could and brought them to the front of the station. He took her hand and practically dragged her with him. He ran through the station, holding more tightly to Lillian than he ever had before. He wished he didn't have to let go so soon.

The train steamed, and Samuel threw his pack on the train car. The conductor looked at him with slight irritation. The wheels began to turn, and he let his hand fall on Lillian's waist once again, drawing her close and hugging her tightly. "I'll come home," he whispered.

He kissed her hand the way so many other men had, but held it close, knowing now she was only his. He turned and entered his train car as the whistle blew. He waved out the open window.

"I love you, Lily," he called as the train lurched forward.

"I love you, Sam." She giggled. "If you don't write me before you come home next, I'll kill you." She touched one hand to her lips and waved to him.

The train pulled away, and he watched Lillian walk closer to the edge of the platform so he could see her until the last moment. The train carried on, and Samuel's eyes stayed on her until his new fiancé was out of sight. He leaned his head back on the seat of the train and laughed to himself. He felt more joyous and more free returning to the trenches than he had in all his life. He pulled one sheet and one envelope from Lillian's parcel.

My Lily,

I've just left you, and it's so strange I took so long to say what we both always knew was true. Thank you for always being braver than me. You have always been the soldier for us—fighting all the time for us to have a life together, even if neither of us knew what it would be. I think we just ensured what Daniel told me—the world won't be the same when this is over. Thank God for that. I love you, Lily. I'll make it home to you—however long it takes.

Until then, I'll be sending all my love, from the trenches, to you.

Yours always,
Samuel

EPILOGUE

Two years later: June 4, 1917

Lillian sat at the small table in the Perry home and smiled at Anna and Nellie. Even though the war had not ended and the future was still uncertain, she was in total bliss. Nellie stood behind her, happily pinning Lillian's hair back into a low bun with pieces framing her face and falling down in places the way she liked. The two girls giggled while Anna Perry stitched and mended a white gown in the chair opposite them.

"It's almost finished," she said, working carefully on the hem.

"Oh, Anna, it'll be lovely. You've already done so much for me," Lillian said, smiling.

"Well, I couldn't very well let you stay on the street when your parents knew you wouldn't change your mind," she said, returning the smile.

Lillian reached for Anna Perry's hand and squeezed it. She leaned back, thinking over the last two years since Samuel's proposal. Her parents had been disappointed but not shocked. They had made living in the Harlow household unbearable—begging her to change her mind at every turn. But she never relented. She wouldn't let him go again. So they disinherited her—told her to leave—and Anna Perry gave her a home. Truly, it was the home she always wanted to share. Nellie's bedroom had become her small haven, and John had come to share in its tranquility often. His wheelchair had been swapped for crutches when his shame was traded for acceptance. Remembering the kindness of her new family drew tears from deep within her, but she smiled through them—thanking Anna Perry with every look.

Nellie pulled back Lillian's shoulders to square them with the chair. "Lillian, if you want your hair done for your wedding day, I suggest you sit still," she joked, shooing the tears away.

"Yes, Nurse Perry," she said, joking back. "And don't forget, you're wearing that dress," she added, pointing through the door to a lavender dress that lay on her bed.

"Lily, I couldn't. It's one of the best dresses you have, and I—"

"Deserve it. You're almost twenty-three. You're a talented nurse. You've worked relentlessly for years now. You deserve one day of pretty dresses and some fun. Let today be that day for you, please. It will be your wedding gift to me—and I'm sure your brother would like it too."

"Fine, if you insist." Nellie finally relented. "But only because I love you so very much," she said, hugging Lillian from behind—attempting to not ruin the hair she had just finished pinning.

"There now—finished," Anna Perry said, holding up Lillian's wedding dress. The white dress was the most extravagant thing she owned now. It dripped in lace, and its back hung from her shoulders, leaving the top of her back exposed. There were small, embroidered flowers throughout the lace, and it was by far the loveliest thing Lillian had ever seen. Nellie and Anna helped her dress and hung her veil cap on top of her head and let the train flow down over her dark curls. Then the Perrys went to dress, leaving Lillian alone with her thoughts for a moment. A knock came at the door.

"Don't come in! It's bad luck," Lillian yelled.

"Samuel Perry, don't you dare!" Nellie said, running from her room while fastening the final button on her dress.

"Calm down, girls. It's me." James' voice shouted behind the door. "I've come to check on my investment."

Lillian laughed. "Let him in, Nel."

Nellie opened the door to James standing in his uniform proudly. He caught Lillian's gaze, and she watched her brother's eyes glisten ever so slightly.

"Well?" Lillian asked, turning to one side and the other.

"Well, the dress is lovely, but you are lovelier. I'm glad I could do it for you. You deserved a wonderful dress, even if I didn't have quite enough money saved to give you the perfect wedding."

"Oh, I didn't need all that," she said, moving toward him and taking his hands. "The dress was more than enough. I never did like the idea of a big society wedding. A little wedding in the church with a small meal is perfectly lovely."

"But you deserved it. And they're absolutely rotten for not giving it to you. I'll give you all you need when I inherit. You know that, don't you?" he asked, holding her hand tightly.

"I do. You don't need to, but I know you will anyway. I love you for it." Lillian hugged her brother and released him when Anna Perry reentered.

"It's almost time. Nellie, run ahead and fetch our seats. James, you go wait outside for Lillian." Nobody dared question Anna Perry, and soon Lillian stood alone with her almost mother-in-law. She watched as Anna slipped the small gold band off her left hand.

"Oh, Anna, I—"

"I don't want to hear anything about it. I'll be giving this to Albert before the ceremony begins to give to Samuel when it's time. He'll know where it came from, but I wanted you to know too," she said.

Lillian bent down and kissed her cheek. "Thank you—for everything."

Anna Perry exited in a hurry while James entered again and handed her the bouquet of pale pink peonies and lilies of the valley.

"Are you ready?"

Lillian laughed. "I've been ready for so long."

She took her brother's arm, and he led her out the door and down the short walk to the small church. It held only a few people, but everyone she needed was there. Her brother and her stood outside, arm in arm, until the music began. "I'm happy it's you giving me away, James. Thank you for doing it."

Her brother nodded and kissed her cheek, and they stepped forward into the church.

Samuel stood at the end of the aisle with Albert. How they both managed to receive leave, she would never know. Samuel was Major Perry now, so she was certain he took care of things. Her soldier smiled at her, and she knew in that moment everything she had risked and lost for him didn't matter.

Lillian held tightly to James as they finally made it to the end of the aisle. She offered her cheek to James, who kissed it before placing her hand in Samuel's. She hesitated a moment, feeling freed by the ability to finally touch him in public without fear of discovery or shame. She smiled at him, tears already beginning.

Lillian attempted to pay attention and remember every second that made up her wedding day. But the spoken words faded into the background as she stared at Samuel Perry and reminded herself it was not a dream. She said her vows in a daze and hardly heard Samuel's, but in her heart, she knew they both meant every piece of them. She laughed through tears as Samuel slid Anna Perry's ring on her left hand and wept a little harder as he revealed his father's ring for her to slide onto his—and she did with all her heart.

* * *

The afternoon bled into evening as the few guests sat at a table that had been brought outside the Perry home. Lillian hadn't touched a bite but instead wandered among the people who made up her life and smiled. Samuel grinned at her from across the small crowd, and Lillian marveled at how life had changed. Lillian's thoughts were broken when Nellie rushed at her from the house.

"Lily, someone is here for you. He's outside. He says he won't interrupt and come to the back."

Suddenly, Lillian realized whose presence was missing, and she removed her veil and retraced Nellie's steps through the house. Outside the Perry house, she met Jonah Winlen.

"Jonah," she said, and he turned to face her.

"Lillian," he said, smiling. "You look beautiful."

"Please come through. We want you here," she said, tugging his arm.

"I assume you're being polite and not sincere, but when I received the invitation, I thought it rude to not make an appearance," he said kindly but decidedly.

"If it wasn't for you, this day might not have come. I'm not sure how kind that is, but it's true. Thank you for that," she said.

"Lily, Samuel's looking for you." Nellie appeared, breaking the silence after Lillian's gratitude. Lillian nodded and turned back to Jonah, who looked past her now.

"Perhaps I should at least greet the groom," he said, offering Lillian his arm. The pair followed Nellie back outside, and Lillian switched escorts as they arrived at Samuel's side.

"Captain Winlen. Nice of you to come," Samuel said, extending his hand.

"Actually, it's Major now. Thank you, Second Lieutenant Perry," Jonah answered, staying stationary.

"I'm also a Major now. Thank you," Samuel snapped back, lowering his hand. The two men stared at each other, accepting their position in life and in rank.

"Congratulations to you both—truly," Jonah said, releasing his stiffness and showing sincerity.

"Thank you, Jonah. Nellie," Lillian called, catching her new sister's attention. "Won't you show Major Winlen where he can find a drink?"

Nellie nodded in understanding—which Lillian was thankful for—as she led Jonah away.

Lillian stood alone with Samuel, holding his arm and smiling. "It was nice of him to come, wasn't it, Sam?"

"Yes, I suppose it was, Mrs. Perry," he said, smiling and pulling her closer. She giggled at her new name.

"It was nice of all of them, really."

"You're not sorry your parents aren't here?" he asked.

She shook her head.

Her eyes flitted over the crowd. John stood tall for the first time in a long time. James seemed almost content with the life he would inherit someday. Nellie was more a woman than ever before—standing with a glass of champagne and a man in uniform. Her whole life lay in front of her eyes, and Lillian loved each part of it.

"No, I think I'm quite happy, Samuel. I wish Daniel were here, but I think he knew somehow."

"That strange Christmas in the trench—it made me think he knew too," he agreed. "But you're sure you're happy? No turning back now, you know." He laughed.

"I assure you I have no desire to turn back." And finally, Lillian kissed her husband, her soldier, her love—the gardener boy.

ACKNOWLEDGMENTS

While writing a book of my own has been a dream I've had since my childhood, it would be foolish to believe this dream come true belongs only to me.

I would like to thank the following people:

My parents—for dreaming all my dreams with me and never faltering in their support.

My brother—for picking me up every step of the way and providing me with an endless supply of empty journals to fill over the years.

My sister-in-law—for being one of the best supporters and cheerleaders.

The Huntington University history department—for being a safe home away from home to dig into the past and find my future.

The Huntington University English department—for strengthening my craft and pushing me further into literature.

Emily VanderBent and Alyssa Dixon—the first ones to hear almost anything I write and chase away the doubts.

Abby Gruendyke and Hannah King—for believing in me since childhood and cheering me on from wherever they are.

Eric Koester—for teaching me the most effective way to make my dream a reality.

Brian Bies—for helping me make my book the best it could be.

Clayton Bohle—for cutting through the first draft with me and making it better.

Rebecca Bruckenstein—for pushing me, supporting me, and cheering me on throughout the journey.

And for each person who preordered *All My Love, From the Trenches.* You were the first ones to believe in this story, and for that, I'm eternally grateful.

Steve and Cheryl Vore
The Goble Family
Damon Richardson
Bryanna Smith
Alyssa Dixon
Grant Fleming
Abigail Gruendyke
Maggie McLaughlin
Sheila Weiland
Roberta Kroll
Debra Kowalkowski
Carie King
Sarah Holt
Shelby Kochel
Ali Everett
Shannon Koga
Hannah King
Tom Rogers
Marissa Miller
Allison Millspaugh
Renee Glass
Sheila Johnson
Jessika Rucker
Elizabeth Maki
Marva Martz
Gail Vore
Mark Dold
Emily Craig
Kenny Heiniger
Lynn Deetz
Margo Takehara
Isaac Hatch
Tony Haisley
Haley Newlin
Gary and Barb VanderBent
Tawny Hinrichsen
Karen Wolf
Carter Lloyd
Michele Lazard
Tim and April VanderBent
Brett Holder
The Bagley Family
Jan King
Faith Hill
Abbey Frisco
Nathan Fosnough

Hannah Seward
Jordyn Macbeth
Ashley Onken
Ali Williams
Michelle Fouts
Amanda Schmucker
Melody Schmucker
Daniel Dixon
Gina Schmucker
Lori Ernsberger
Emily VanderBent
Kierstin Leavitt
Andrew Esch
Jennifer Lucas
Eric Koester
Andrew Freer
Nancy Van Gessel
Meredith Oliver
Jacob and Kelsie Vore
Abigail Field
Mina Craw
Maddy Burkholder
Brendan Wallace
Pam Harrison
Mandi Smith
Rob Neel
Melissa DeBoliac
Allan Simon
Andrew Bower
Dawn Downing
Jackie Lucas
Alec Boyd-Devine
Savannah Olson
Mandy Prater
Jenna King
Cathy Trout
Margaret Gruendyke
Allison Gill
Patti Swets
Trevor Morgan
Jill Thurman
Dennis Smith
Julia Walton
Susie Martin
Colleen Yordy
Amber VanderBent
Betty Willman
Terri Collins
Rochelle Herge
Robyn Lynn Fox
Robyn Lynn Groves
Sharon Buckler
Shayla Herron
Brittany Sisson
Shane Banning
Bethany Miller
Brent Simon
Jamie Conrad

CPSIA information can be obtained
at www.ICGtesting.com
Printed in the USA
LVHW022329120423
744251LV00024B/495